Chris Hammonds was born in Wolverhampton, in 1943, studied Spanish and Portuguese at Bristol University, and Linguistics at the University of Leeds. He worked as an academic in Sweden, Slovenia, Romania and Norway. He has lectured in China, Croatia, Spain and Thailand, and worked as a radio producer and broadcaster at the BBC World Service. His book: *English Pronunciation OK!* has been translated into a number of languages.

Chris has run several marathons, and in 2006 he competed in the Ironman World Championships in Florida. He regularly plays tennis, badminton, table tennis and chess. He has three children and eight grandchildren.

To Mason, Bay, Freya, Matilda, Tristan, Luna, Neo and Violet.

And to all the other grandchildren of the world.

Christopher Hammonds

DODGSON'S DODO

AUSTIN MACAULEY PUBLISHERS™

LONDON • CAMBRIDGE • NEW YORK • SHARJAH

A CIP catalogue record for this title is available from the British Library.

ISBN 9781398442573 (Paperback)
ISBN 9781398442580 (Hardback)
ISBN 9781398442597 (ePub e-book)

www.austinmacauley.com

First Published 2022
Austin Macauley Publishers Ltd®
1 Canada Square
Canary Wharf
London
E14 5AA

Special thanks to Alex for so much practical help, for suggestions and for inspiring the cover design; to Mariel for many useful comments, and to both of them for their wonderful encouragement. Thanks also to Emeritus Professor John C. Wilcox, Anne Kendall, Elza Scott and Hilary Soms for prompting me to publish. And to Dinah Monnickendam and Bobby Cadwallader for their support.

Chapter One

'Imagine what they'd say!'

'Who? People?'

'Yes, people. Just imagine what they'd say!'

Every December, at the beginning of December to be precise, there is a gathering in a wood on a gentle slope, a place where people sometimes walk in summer, but where few come in the winter, for the undergrowth is wet and slippery from fallen leaves, the soil is heavy from the autumn rains and the views are often veiled in mist. This is a place where woodland birds and the shy, quiet animals of England's countryside go about, the birds hopping here and fluttering there, the animals foraging and burrowing and creeping around in their mysterious little ways. Sometimes they call to each other, warning of danger or just making contact, in the way that birds and animals do, have probably always done and will almost certainly continue to do until time stops and a different order comes about in this strange and wonderful universe.

The December gathering is an unusual event, for it brings together four friends whose paths don't normally cross, and nobody remembers how it all started. The kingfisher, for example, is a bird which is typically to be found perched above the flowing waters of the river or skimming along, inches above the surface, showing off its iridescent beauty to those lucky enough to see it, and yet, here it is, visiting a wood a good half-mile from its usual haunts, further from the sound of water than it would ever be if it were not for this annual meeting. The rook, another member of the group, is more at home in this damp woodland spot – in fact, his actual home is within earshot, so to speak. Of course, we all know that homes are more likely to be within sight than earshot, but with rooks, it's the other way round. You hear the home of a rook before you see it, for rooks are loud birds and they live together with family and friends high in the trees, and they cackle and they argue and they squawk as if the business of life is all about showing each other and telling the rest of the world that you and your buddies can make an awful lot of noise, through the day and well into the evening.

The blackbird and the owl both live in the wood, though at opposite ends, the owl at the higher end, from where he can keep a watchful eye on the mice and the voles as they scamper about between the trees at night, while the blackbird prefers to live at the bottom end with its view of the open fields just beyond the trees. Anyway, that's the group of friends, unlikely as it may seem and, as I said, they meet up in early December every year without fail. And the reason? Oh, that's simple: they need to decide what presents they want to give and receive on Christmas Day. How can I explain? Well, you know how you get a pretty good idea of your neighbours' habits after living next door to them for a year or two. It's a bit like that with birds. They've been next door to us humans for millennia, so they know a thing or two about how we live our lives. Our British birds have picked up the idea of

Christmas in the same way that I imagine Indian birds will have absorbed the essentials of Hindu culture and customs, while the birds of Arabia will be familiar with the rituals and festivals of Islam. Stands to reason, really! As for the migrating birds, they have the best of both worlds, knowing all about the cultures of Europe and Africa, or North and South America. Multicultural birds we should call them, I suppose.

So, to come back to our wood and December's meeting. Let's just listen in for a bit, shall we?

'Imagine what humans would say if they knew we had Christmas, just like them,' said Owl, who was aware that he had a reputation for wisdom, and always took it upon himself to 'perch' the meetings, as it were.

'They'd never believe it,' croaked Rook, who seemed bad-tempered, but wasn't really. It's just the way he sounded, what with that gruff voice of his.

'Well,' piped Kingfisher, 'I vote we get the meeting going so that I can be back home in time for lunch. It's alright for you three, you all live in and around these parts, but my larder's right down there in the river at the bottom of the hill and I can't hang about too long so, with respect, can we get started please?'

Owl swivelled his head and blinked that slow, disdainful blink – so specifically owlish, and declared the meeting open.

'I declare the meeting open,' he said in a voice which seemed rather more lugubrious than the occasion required, but that was Owl and nothing was likely to change his style, not even the prospect of Christmas.

'I have some views I would like to share about the gifts we presented and received last Christmas,' sang Blackbird, always an elegant communicator, but sometimes quietly criticised by the others for being more interested in style than content. However, they all listened, showed due respect and awaited the views of Blackbird which, on this occasion, turned out to have a good deal of content. He pronounced as follows:

'It's my sincere wish that no offence will be caused by the words which I intend to utter.' (He did have a tendency to prefer twenty words where half a dozen would be quite adequate, and if a ballot had been taken, Kingfisher, for one, would have voted for the half dozen.)

'Come on, Blackbird,' she piped, 'we haven't got all day!'

'Er, order!' said Owl, nodding his prodigious head in the direction of the diminutive kingfisher, who was the only female in the group, and far and away the best looking of them all. She tossed her dainty little head in a manner that implied haughtiness and naughtiness in roughly equal measure.

'To continue,' sang Blackbird, seemingly undeterred by the interruptions, 'not, as I was saying, wishing to offend anyone, I would like to propose that, instead of imitating humans, as we have in the past, we follow our own instincts – which, as you all know, we are blessed with in abundance. If I may be permitted to give an example…'

'Please be brief,' said Owl, while Rook looked on with a sharp and beady eye.

'Last Christmas I received a yo-yo,' sang Blackbird. 'Rook was given a Rubik's cube and, if my memory serves me well, you, Owl, were the recipient of a hula hoop. Kingfisher, as always, was presented with some kind of make-up.'

'What's your point?' croaked Rook.

'My point is the following,' sang Blackbird. 'A yo-yo, a Rubik's cube, a hula hoop and make-up are all human creations and, as such, are not in essence suited to our avian manner of living, or "lifestyle" as humans are wont to call it. I mean, what is the purpose behind gifting a hula hoop to our dear and respected friend Owl when it's plain to see that he has no discernible waist around which to spin the wretched thing.'

'Blackbird has a point,' said Owl, closing one eye, creating the impression that the other eye was open wider than ever, as though glowering imperiously through a monocle. 'Try as I might, I never actually managed to master the hoop and I spent all my time picking it up and attempting to wiggle the hips which, in truth, I haven't really got. Most frustrating!'

'Well,' croaked Rook, 'in all honesty, I have to confess that I had great trouble with the Rubik's cube. I knew what to do, but I couldn't actually do it single-footed. It took three of us – my cousin, a friend and me, using our feet and our beaks to turn the sections round so that we could get the patterns in the right order. We did it in the end, but it wasn't the ideal present for a bird, truth to tell. The chess set I got the year before was a much better gift, though I really do wish those humans would desist from calling a castle a rook, as so many of them do. It looks like a castle, so why call it a rook?'

'Er, I think we're digressing a little,' said Owl. 'What do you think, Kingfisher?'

'Well,' she fluttered her feathers to shake off some imaginary drops of water, a nervous tick she seemed to have, but charming and very feminine in its way. 'My feeling is that in this day and age I should not be given make-up every year, as if that's the only thing a girl's interested in. After all, I've got a brain in my head, maybe not quite as big as yours, Owl, or yours, Rook, but make-up, lovely as it is, should not be the *only* present I get. Maybe make-up plus something else would be more suitable for the twenty-first century.' She gave another sexy little shake of her feathers and Owl winked at Rook, whose eyes had a very knowing twinkle.

'If I may make my suggestion,' sang Blackbird in his beautifully cadenced manner. 'I'd like to propose that we give personalised presents to each other this year and in future years, and I'd also like to suggest that we invite other birds to join us in our festive celebrations.'

'Er, one thing at a time, if you please,' said Owl, asserting his authority with his usual firm politeness. 'Er, what precisely do you mean by personalised presents?' he enquired.

'Well,' sang Blackbird, ' I would like to imagine that I'm living until next Christmas with Rook's brain instead of my own, because everyone knows that Rook and his fellow crows are the most intelligent birds of all, and I would love to spend twelve months experiencing some of that intelligence.'

'You flatter me, Blackbird,' croaked Rook. 'I've heard it said that parrots are pretty smart, too, but I suppose if we're talking about England my family, that is, the crow family, us rooks and ravens and so on, we are supposed to be up there with the brightest, so I guess you're right. Thanks, anyway. Much appreciated!' He looked across at Owl, but Owl seemed a bit put out. He'd always thought wisdom was a pretty clever thing to have, especially when combined with age, but he bit his little tongue and desisted from protestation, deciding that silence was more dignified than an argument about who was the smartest.

'So exactly how would you go about imagining you had Rook's intelligence?' said Owl, twisting his head slowly and effortlessly towards Blackbird.

'Well, that's where the spirit of Christmas comes in,' sang Blackbird, mellifluous as ever. 'Rook will spend time with me, explaining how his intelligence works, giving me an insight into his view of the world. It'll be an educational experience, and Rook will gain pleasure from sharing his knowledge while I will enhance my ability to solve problems and confront the vicissitudes of life in our little woodland.'

Rook was immediately won over by Blackbird's eloquently expressed proposal, and enthused with some extremely noisy croaks.

'Alright,' said Owl. 'I can see what's in it for you, Blackbird, and if Rook is happy with the idea of giving – an important aspect of Christmas after all, I can understand how he'll benefit, but what about the rest of us? How can this work for us?'

'Easy,' sang Blackbird. 'Let me recapitulate first. Rook imparts some of his intelligence to me. He gives, I receive. At the same time, he can imagine he has a beautiful song for the year, a song like mine. I'll show him my melodies and he'll do his best to imitate. If his voice can't manage it, his brain will help him to understand the music – rather like Beethoven when he went deaf. He could still hear the music in his head even though his ears were useless. As for you and Kingfisher, why don't you do an imaginary swap of one of your abilities for the year? For example, you, Owl, could show Kingfisher how you manage to sleep in the day and hunt at night, and she could show you how to fly over the water at breakneck speed. You could even try eating fish, to see if you like it, and

Kingfisher might sample a bit of mouse, just for the experience. We can all learn from each other, and that could be our gift for Christmas. What do you think? What do the rest of you think?'

'I think it's brilliant,' piped Kingfisher.

'Me, too,' croaked Rook.

'Well. We can certainly give it a try,' said Owl, 'and see how it goes for a year. And didn't you say something about inviting others to join us?' he added, rotating his head back towards Blackbird.

'Absolutely,' sang Blackbird, 'but we'd have to meet in the summer to catch some of them. For instance, I'd love to find out about life in Africa from one of those birds that visit us in the summer, the swifts or the swallows or the cuckoos.'

'Er, not the cuckoos,' said Owl, scowling as only an owl can scowl. 'Cuckoos are not really very nice. They don't have any moral values.'

'Oh yes, they do,' piped Kingfisher. 'They love their babies. They arrange foster care for them and everything.'

'Foster care!' screeched Owl, losing his decorum as his sense of outrage took brief possession of his emotions. 'Foster care! Is that what you call it! I call it colonisation, *and* the murder of innocents, *and* deception, *and* fraud and…and… er…'

'If I may?' croaked Rook. Owl nodded his permission, relieved to be spared the need to find more words to categorise the conduct of cuckoos. 'If I may,' repeated Rook. 'I think we would all agree that cuckoos are a law unto themselves and that their childcare arrangements are, well, eccentric…um, no, correction, um, dubious, but isn't Christmas about being kind and understanding and forgiving, so maybe we should be charitable even towards cuckoos, and next time we come across one perhaps we could give him a chance to defend himself, or herself, to give us their point of view, and then we can pass judgment after a proper debate.'

'Well spoken, Rook,' piped Kingfisher.

'Wise words,' sang Blackbird.

'I suppose you have a point,' said Owl, acknowledging Rook's facility with words and the power of his crow brain. 'And it would appear to be the view of all members that we should adopt Blackbird's proposal for the exchange of presents this year.'

They all nodded, as one.

'Now,' said Owl, 'does anyone else wish to raise a matter or make a proposal before I close the meeting?'

'I think Blackbird has given us all plenty to think about for the time being,' croaked Rook, 'so I, for one, have nothing more to add.'

'Same here,' piped Kingfisher, who hadn't entirely forgotten about her larder in the river and about the lunch which no doubt awaited her there.

Blackbird, who normally took a back seat in the meetings, content to go along with whatever the others proposed, was well-pleased with the reception given to his uncharacteristic and rather radical suggestion, so he merely nodded to the others – first Owl, then Rook and finally Kingfisher, by way of acknowledgement of their gracious acceptance of his proposal.

'So,' said Owl, 'before I declare the meeting closed, I would like to take this opportunity of wishing you, in advance, a Merry Christmas, one and all.'

'And a very Merry Christmas, Owl, to you too,' they sang, piped and croaked in a hearty chorus, with warm, "birdy" smiles in their eyes. (Their beaks, of course, were far too rigid to manage anything as sinuous as a smile, but the eyes seemed to cope reasonably well, so happiness was able to radiate quite successfully, in keeping with the season of festivity.)

Chapter Two

Christmas came and went, New Year passed, snow fell and eventually melted, the trees stood up to the winter winds and before long Nature was marking the arrival of spring. There were all the usual signs: as far as Owl was concerned there were more hours for sleep and fewer for hunting; for Kingfisher the fish were out and about, just waiting to be picked off and savoured, while in the woods brand new leaves, crispy clean and perfectly formed, were appearing on the trees.

Rook made a few repairs to his nest, and Blackbird went up-market, his mate having decided that they were moving to a more desirable location in which to raise the anticipated family. The new site was well within singing distance of last season's nest, but there could be no doubt about its superiority. Blackbird's partner had scouted around for many days before settling for a fine-looking hawthorn. Very soon she'd be building a homely nest high in the branches. From here there would be a commanding view of the surrounding countryside, but more significantly, security would be much better than in last year's rather run-down neighbourhood, where there had been an influx of sparrows which, everyone agreed, had lowered the tone of the area. "Such common birds" was a phrase that seemed to be on every beak. Blackbird was delighted with the new location and proud of having chosen such a diligent partner.

Rook was circling above the wood, for no particular reason and, feeling slightly dizzy after the twentieth circle (or was it even the thirtieth?) he drifted down and settled on a branch where, quite by chance, his old friend Owl happened to be snoozing. Owl awoke, startled by the intrusion, but he quickly composed himself and was soon in conversation with his sleek and glossy neighbour.

'Haven't seen you for a while,' said Owl.

'I know,' croaked Rook. 'I've been busy up at the rookery. Every spring we all work at fixing our nests ready for the new season. It gets quite competitive, really, with everyone trying to use the best twigs to make their nest stronger and better than all the others. There's a lot to do after the battering of the winter storms, so that's why you won't have seen me around very much.'

'I see,' said Owl, fixing Rook with his huge amber eyes. 'Have you heard about Blackbird? He's moving house with his partner after those new neighbours settled in…you know, the sparrows.'

'Yes, I heard rumours. I'm sure they'll be happy in their new place, once she's built it. Did I tell you my partner and I are planning a family very soon, so you won't be seeing much of me in the next few weeks either because I'll be providing food for my good lady before the eggs are laid, to make sure she's fit and healthy and all set for motherhood. It's an old custom we have in the rook community. The man of the nest finds food for his mate during the perinatal period.'

'Most laudable! What a splendid example of fatherhood, to say nothing of standards and family values,' said Owl, clearly impressed with Rook's sense of responsibility. 'Which reminds me of another, related matter,' he added in a rather sombre tone.

'Oh yes, and what would that be?' croaked Rook, suspecting from Owl's demeanour that something portentous was about to be revealed.

'Well, I don't quite know how to put this, but it's…it's er, it's about Kingfisher.'

'Oh dear,' croaked Rook. 'Is she not well? I must admit I haven't seen her since we had our meeting in December. Although, having said that, our flight paths rarely cross, what with me living up there in the rookery and her spending all her time down by the river. Different as cheese and chalk we are, Kingfisher and me, I suppose you could say. Here I am, always dressed in black while she's all decked out in that multi-coloured finery of hers and…'

'Er, if I may interrupt,' said Owl, anxious to share his concerns with Rook, and fearful that his friend was falling victim to verbiage, an affliction to which Owl was known to have a very limited tolerance, where it occurred in others, at least. 'The thing is, I've been told that Kingfisher is spending all her time in flirtatious activity with some young newcomer to the area and, well, birds are beginning to talk.'

'Oh that,' croaked Rook. 'So the gossips are out and about are they, being holier than thou are they? Well, Owl, let me tell you something. Young Kingfisher with all her flightiness and lack of constancy is the face of the future. You and I, with our "mating for life" attitude, are probably doomed. You see, we're not stirring the gene pool enough, whereas young

Kingfisher is really mixing it all up – a new partner every year, new genes being spread around all over the place. I'm sure that Darwin fellow said something about it. "Survival of the flightiest" was one of his phrases, if I'm not mistaken.'

'So you don't think Kingfisher is giving us all a bad name, then?' said Owl, who certainly knew Darwin, but was not entirely au fait with the niceties of "natural selection" except that, from a purely personal point of view, he believed that his selection of his partner had seemed quite natural and their relationship, though not exactly effervescent, was, without doubt, steady and mutually respectful.

'I think Kingfisher is absolutely fine,' croaked Rook who, truth to tell, had always had a bit of a soft spot for their little friend, who was, indeed, as pretty as the proverbial picture. 'She's just doing what kingfishers have always done, and as a species, it has to be admitted that they're very successful. They're not called kingfishers for nothing. Kings of fishing, that's what they are, and they're all over the world, hunting and flirting with all the enthusiasm and joie de vivre of a French king.'

'Goodness,' said Owl, 'I had no idea you were such a fan. And here was I worrying about scandal instead of embracing promiscuity as the saviour of us all!' He lifted one of his talons, lowered his head and scratched. Then he blinked, very slowly, twice. He had a puzzled look, but then owls often do! He spoke again. 'On reflection, wasn't it promiscuity and joie de vivre and too much hunting and flirting that led to a certain French king losing his head? Or have I misunderstood something?'

'Oh, the French!' croaked Rook. 'No, we mustn't generalise from the French. Indeed no! They're a bit like our friends the cuckoos – a law unto themselves. But no, I think you have Louis XIV, the so-called "Sun King", in mind, but it wasn't *he* who lost his head. No, no, the unfortunate victim of Madame la Guillotine was not number 14 but number 16, a king who allowed himself to be dominated by his queen, a certain Marie Antoinette, and it was her reputation for extravagance that helped provoke the French Revolution. The economy was in a mess and we all know that with humans when the economy is in a mess there's likely to be unrest. The Americans, universally noted for their linguistic subtlety and oratorical flourishes, have a typically manicured phrase to sum it up: "It's the economy, stupid!"'

Owl listened most attentively to Rook's own display of language and noted his familiarity with continental history. He inwardly smiled at the reference to the French and he prided himself on picking up Rook's ironic swipe at the Americans. He swivelled his head to the very limit of its rotation as if to check that what he was about to say would not be overheard by any other creature. His head slowly unwound itself on its hidden pivot until it was back to its starting point and then, after a moment of reflection, he proceeded to address his friend with the following thoughts and observations:

'Rook, you really are a most knowledgeable bird. I sometimes question my own reputation for wisdom when I compare myself with you. I am, occasionally, tortured by self-doubt, worrying that that adjective so readily and, it would seem, universally attributed to me, namely: "wise", is perhaps just another example of humans doing what they habitually insist on doing.' He peered deep into Rook's shiny black eyes. 'I can see that you know exactly what I'm about to say.'

'Anthropomorphism,' croaked Rook without a moment's hesitation.

'The very word,' said Owl. 'As I'm sure you know, all over England there are pictures of me outside colleges of education and universities wearing a gown and a mortarboard. And it's all because I look serious and, well…'

'All-seeing,' croaked Rook. 'It's the eyes, dear friend, the eyes. It's that penetrating gaze. That's what it is. It makes you look perceptive – the very epitome of perceptiveness. And the magnificent style of your blink just adds a touch of exoticism. Humans love it – a touch of exoticism. It's all about your eyes, my friend, and yet the ability which should impress beyond all others is your facility to rotate that noble head of yours a wondrous 270 degrees without constricting your arteries and stopping the blood flow to your brain. Any other bird attempting such a thing would suffer a fatal stroke. Your neck-swivelling is a feat unsurpassed in all of nature – well, amongst us birds, anyway. That's what really singles you out but, for the humans, it's the eyes. No doubt about it.' And with that, Rook closed his beak and nodded his jet-coloured head in obvious approval – a gesture of self-congratulation at his own appraisal of the facts regarding his friend's status among humans. Unexpectedly, his beak opened again, as if an afterthought had suddenly occurred to him. 'Pandas,' he croaked.

'I beg your pardon?' said Owl.

'Pandas. Giant pandas. They suffer from something similar.'

'What on earth do you mean?' said Owl, blinking his left eye while the other remained focused on Rook's formidable beak.

'What I mean is that humans are attracted to other creatures which have big eyes set in big round faces. You owls have big eyes in round faces and so do pandas. Well not exactly, but it seems so. Pandas' eyes aren't particularly large, but they are set in big black furry circles, which look like eyes, so humans love them. It's the same with their babies.'

'You mean pandas' babies?' said Owl, beginning to get a little confused by all this anthropomorphism and its ramifications.

'No, don't get me started on pandas and their babies,' croaked Rook who, for no obvious reason suddenly did a rather fancy bit of footwork along the branch they were perched on. He took a couple of paces to the right and an equally nimble couple of steps back again.

'Now you've lost me,' said Owl. 'I really have no idea what you're talking about.'

'Sometimes I despair of humans,' croaked Rook. 'They're so superficial. The things they do are often so stupid, so sentimental, so lacking in common sense. Just consider what they've done with pandas. We're talking here of an animal that has evolved so foolishly that it can eat bamboo and nothing but bamboo, and which is almost incapable of reproducing. The female is hardly ever fertile – two days a year! I ask you! And the male is, well, how can I put it in polite terminology, er…inadequate. And yet, humans have put the panda on the world wildlife pedestal, and all because it's got a cute round face with the appearance of big black eyes. I mean, how shallow can you get!'

Owl was staring into the far distance, assimilating Rook's pronouncements and wondering what the implications were for his own relationship with humans. Without warning, Rook started up again.

'When I said, "It's the same with their babies," I was referring to human babies. I was about to say that humans find their own babies irresistible because they have big eyes in round faces, just like you and pandas. Human eyes are the only part of their bodies that hardly grow, so they are almost adult size at birth, which makes them big in relation to the size of the face, and babies usually have chubby round faces for the first months of their lives, so humans love them, which, of course, is good for the babies because although they make the most frightful smells and messes, and demand constant feeding and attention, and prevent their parents from sleeping for weeks at a time, their attractive eyes and faces hypnotise the parents and make them attentive to their every need.' Rook sighed a croakish sort of sigh and dropped his head, as if exhausted by the effort of explaining everything in such detail to his friend Owl, who sometimes seemed to Rook to be surprisingly ill-informed about so many worldly things, despite his reputation for wisdom.

The two friends sat in silence for several minutes and then, as if by the waving of a wand, Blackbird appeared.

'Hello, you two,' he sang, cheery as always. 'I was told you were here so I thought I'd pop by and say "How d'ya do".'

'Hello,' said Owl.

'How d'ya do?' croaked Rook.

There was a brief pause, then:

'How are you two getting on with your Christmas presents?' asked Owl, reminded of the December agreement by Blackbird's sudden arrival on the branch.

The two black-plumed birds looked at each other, then Blackbird extended one of his wings as an invitation to Rook to speak first.

'After you,' croaked Rook.

'Well, it will be a challenging task to give an honest account without creating the impression that I am a shameless flatterer,' sang Blackbird. Rook looked down at his feet in real or feigned embarrassment. It was hard to tell with a rook, since blushing was out of the question. 'The truth is,' continued Blackbird, 'Rook has been inordinately generous with his time, and has tutored me in the art and science of intelligence with such a degree of patience and such a wonderful command of his subject that if my own analytical skills and powers of deduction have not shown significant signs of improvement since Christmas, it is in no way due to Rook, but is most assuredly and, I might add, regrettably, a reflection of my intellectual limitations as a mere blackbird.'

Rook opened his beak as if to protest at Blackbird's modesty, but Owl was quicker off the mark – unusual for Owl.

'And how about you, Rook? How are the singing lessons coming along?'

Rook scraped his throat and looked as sheepish as it's possible for a bird to look. Unfortunately, any amount of throat scraping is time and effort completely wasted in a rook, for the exhalation of air through the oral cavity of any member of the crow family will always sound like the very antithesis of music, even Hard Rock or Stockhausen. Rook opened his beak but decided to have another scrape of the throat. At least that's what it sounded like, but with a rook, it can be difficult to distinguish between an energetic scraping of the throat and a genuine utterance. Finally, he managed a coherent articulation.

'Blackbird has been inspirational, exemplary in his demonstrations and a very model of clarity in reducing melody to its constituent parts, in illustrating the intricacies of phraseology and rhythmical pattern-making; in short, he has proved to be the perfect music teacher.'

Blackbird looked proud, Owl seemed impressed and Rook feared the worst.

'I hope you are not going to ask me to sing,' he croaked, sounding even more croaky than normal, and looking directly into Owl's inscrutable eyes. 'The truth is, musical appreciation is one thing, but musical talent is quite another. Blackbird has worked wonders on my understanding of the construction and artistry of music, but we have both come to the conclusion that the ability to perform in public is an innate facility – one which Blackbird possesses in orchestral dimensions while I, as a member of the crow family – family Corvidae, would be unworthy even to attempt a minor role in the percussion section of an amateur band.' And with that, he struck his prodigious beak against the branch on which they were all perched. It was the full stop at the end of his sentence. It was the end of the conversation, or that particular part of the conversation, and it was interpreted as such by all three birds.

Chapter Three

They sat quietly for a while, as if musing on what had been said. It was Blackbird who broke the silence.

'It's not often you'll see the three of us sitting together like this, except at our Christmas meetings, of course.' He was stating the obvious, but stating it with exquisite musicality, as always. That was the thing with Blackbird. Even the most mundane of remarks could seem like a nugget of profundity when set so aesthetically to music. Not so very different from some of the operas of humans, perhaps, where the banal may be rendered interesting or even worthy by the provision of a good melodic accompaniment.

'Why don't we go down to the river and say hello to Kingfisher?' Rook suggested.

'Er, not a good idea,' said Owl, whose policy was to avoid travel during the hours of daylight. The other two looked at him questioningly. 'Er, we could be interrupting something,' he added with a slight reluctance.

'What do you mean, "interrupting something"?' sang Blackbird.

'I believe Owl could be referring to Kingfisher's predilection for the amorous arts,' croaked Rook, attempting to dignify Kingfisher's pursuit of her base instincts by his choice of the flowery phrase and the polysyllabic adjective.

'Do you mean "flirting"?' sang Blackbird, half-pretending naiveté, and cocking his coal-black head towards Owl.

'Er, just so,' said Owl with his customary seriousness.

'Well, why don't I go down on my own and, if I can catch her attention, invite her to join us up here?' sang Blackbird, who was just as fond of their water-loving friend as Rook was.

'Excellent idea,' croaked Rook.

Blackbird looked at Owl, expectantly, as did Rook.

'I see no reason why not,' said Owl, apparently neutral, as usual.

And so it was that Kingfisher joined them, neither she nor Blackbird revealing or even hinting at what she had been engaged in at the moment of Blackbird's appearance at water's edge. She may have been fishing for fish or indeed fishing for the compliments of a suitor, but the secret remained exactly that, a secret, known only to the coy little Kingfisher and the splendidly diplomatic Blackbird.

Many weeks had passed since Rook had last seen Kingfisher, so they exchanged warm greetings and were clearly happy to see each other again. Owl, of course, had met up with Kingfisher on several occasions in the last few months as part of their Christmas agreement. Try as he might, Owl had not been able to acquire a taste for fish, while Kingfisher had found the flavour of mouse quite nauseating, so it had been agreed that diet was not something to be tampered with. Fish were for kingfishers and mice were for owls. It was as simple as that! As for the other part of their Christmas agreement, Kingfisher had at first fretted at the prospect of hunting by night, but Owl had shown his avuncular and caring side in preparing Kingfisher for the adventure and on the two or three occasions when they made their forays in the dark he'd led the way so that Kingfisher wouldn't strain her eyes or collide with some obstruction or other. As instructed, she'd simply followed his tail, flying in his considerable slipstream and, after a few initial moments of panic, adrenalin had taken over and she was in for the thrill, swooping this way and that, swerving between oaks and beeches and doing just what any nocturnal hunter does, though she drew the line at attacking voles or other little wanderers of the night. That would have been a step too far. An innocent bystander would have been quite bewildered at the sight of a kingfisher flying beak to tail with an owl, more than twice her size, through the night-time woods. That would indeed have been headline news in the "Avian Herald" if such a broadsheet had existed. Of course, no such broadsheet did exist, but there was "The Woodland Bugle", a popular tabloid, and there happened to be not one, but two independent observers on one of the nights when Kingfisher and Owl were out on a trial run.

"ROGUE 'FISHER HUNTS OWL" was the "Bugle's" headline the following day. There was a vivid description of an intrepid little kingfisher chasing a terrified owl the length and breadth of the woods. There were several references to David and Goliath and much speculation about the eventual outcome of the hunt. Despite thorough searches of the undergrowth, no owl corpse was discovered and there were no traces of kingfisher pellets on the woodland floor, though no one actually knew if a kingfisher was capable of eating an owl. There were those who scoffed at the very notion of kingfisher pellets but when ornithological sources were consulted, they confirmed that kingfishers, just like owls and many other birds, did sometimes regurgitate parts of their food and leave pellets lying around the place. Not a particularly savoury practice, it has to be said but, as far as the birds were concerned, by no means as indecorous as some of the activities humans get up to, what with nose-picking and colonic irrigation, to say nothing of vomiting in the streets on Saturday nights. Makes a bird shudder just to think of such things! Anyway, the episode of a kingfisher hunting an owl was an event that defied logic, and yet the observers were credible sources who stood by their stories and were quite prepared to swear oaths to that effect.

Imagine the chattering and the chirruping, the squeaking and the grunting which accompanied every encounter between the various birds and animals of the woodland in the days following that startling headline in the paper. The creatures, the furry ones as well as the feathery ones, were in turmoil. What might be the implications of such a reversal of the natural order to which they were all accustomed and by which their lives were ruled?

'An owl being hunted by a kingfisher represents an overturning of the laws which govern every detail of our behaviour,' were the words used by Green Woodpecker, in the staccato delivery which she shared with her great spotted and lesser spotted cousins. All the woodpeckers also had this habit of speaking in a formal and rather verbose manner, and this old-fashioned style combined with the disjointed pronunciation made them the butt of many a joke in the wider bird community. All that head-bashing had turned their brains! That was the general theory, but there was a grudging admiration for their carpentry skills, and the rattling echoes that bounced around the woods when they were at work seemed somehow reassuring to most of the other birds and animals as they went about their own business. Green Woodpecker was addressing Magpie who, after reading the main story in the "Bugle", had spent the day flapping around from branch to branch and bush to bush in a state of panic, squawking with more than her usual sense of urgency. If ever a bird deserved a reputation for over-reaction and histrionics it was Magpie. To say she cried wolf twenty times in a typical day would not be an exaggeration. However, on this particular day, her jitters and cries of alarm were, for once, more or less in harmony with the general mood among the inhabitants of the woodland and beyond.

'What is to be done? What is to be done? Deary me! Can anything be done and if so by whom, and how?' squawked Magpie to Green Woodpecker and to the world at large.

Owl and Kingfisher were so busy making arrangements for the remainder of their Christmas exchange that the gossip and speculation about their night-time behaviour completely passed them by. They were oblivious to it all. They knew nothing of the editorial in the "Bugle", where the editor-in-chief, who also happened to be the proprietor, an elderly fox known for his hard-nosed approach to life and for his unwillingness to let go once he'd got his teeth into a good story, had posed a number of questions concerning the nocturnal events in the woods. Perhaps the most notable question he asked his readers to consider was the possibility that climate change or pollution by humans had reduced the number of fish in the rivers so that kingfishers were no longer able to satisfy their appetites with fish alone, leading them to pursue other creatures, in this case, owls, to provide them with sufficient energy for their needs. It seemed bizarre that such small birds should have such gargantuan requirements but, as every woodland bird and animal was aware, kingfishers were quite a sexy species, and promiscuity only thrives where ample nutrition is available to provide the calorific input for the athletic activity known by humans as "love-making" and by kingfishers as "fun". These were the kinds of thoughts preoccupying Chief Editor Fox and his newspaper colleagues, and these were the topics on every woodland beak and mouth – except the beak of Kingfisher, the so-called villain of the piece, and Owl, the other unwitting protagonist of the drama. The two of them were by now ready and prepared for their final Christmas exchange of skills. Owl was to follow Kingfisher along the river in a daylight display, doing his best to fly within a few inches of the surface of the water, and trying his utmost to dart a little to the left and then to the right in the characteristic style of his dainty little friend.

The day for this momentous fly-past was arranged and Owl partook of a light breakfast before heading down to the river for his early morning rendezvous with Kingfisher. He was, in fact, quite nervous and not as alert as he would like to have been, after a busy night's hunting, but he was keen to acquit himself well, Kingfisher's excellent performance in the woods just a few nights earlier being fresh in his mind. It wasn't a matter of rivalry, but pride certainly came into it as far as Owl was concerned. He felt a considerable burden of responsibility resting uneasily on his incredibly rounded shoulders. After all, as an owl he would, in a way, be representing all owls, and it was well known among other birds that the one thing owls could not abide was losing face. They were a proud species, some would say aloof, with a tendency to look down on others, but this may have been partly due to their general appearance, for which they could not in all fairness be held responsible.

'Good morning, Kingfisher,' said Owl with as firm a voice as he could muster.

'Hello, Owl,' replied Kingfisher in a smiley, welcoming way. Kingfisher knew only too well that Owl had never ventured to the river bank before and realised that he would be, to use a human expression, "out of his comfort zone". She therefore felt it incumbent upon her to be the perfect hostess and, while the opportunity presented itself, to show off her habitat in a relaxed way and in as favourable a light as possible. She would like to have invited Owl to view her sleeping quarters, but her burrow in the river bank was far too small to permit the entry of a bird the size of Owl, even with his bottle-shaped shoulders, so she had to content herself with showing her guest the entrance hole and inviting him to join her on her favourite branch. From here they could survey a considerable stretch of water, and Kingfisher explained her plan to Owl in as much detail as she deemed appropriate, for she wished him to feel reasonably confident without being burdened by peripheral issues. She therefore made reference to the speed of the current, to places where the water might be choppy and to the direction and velocity of the wind.

'We might be seen by other birds, most probably herons or cormorants,' she piped, 'but don't pay them any attention. Keep as close to me as you possibly can, just as I did when we hunted together in the woods last week. Is everything clear?'

'Oh, there's just one thing I'd like to ask,' said Owl, who had made meticulous mental notes of the instructions and meteorological details during Kingfisher's little speech. 'How far are we going to fly and how do we stop?'

Kingfisher laughed, a warm and friendly laugh, mindful that she must not do or say anything to offend her much older guest, who did, after all, have a bit of a reputation for taking umbrage quite easily and who could best be described as "one of the old school", not always familiar with the habits and trends of the younger generation.

'We'll go as far as that willow tree in the distance, the one on the left bank where the river bends to the right. And we'll stop by gliding up a few feet to land on a dead branch that hangs over the water. You won't need to look out for it. Just stick as close as you can to my tail and stay there until you see me swoop up, then prepare for landing. Good luck! Are you ready?'

Owl found his attention momentarily distracted by Kingfisher's use…no, misuse…no, in truth, abuse of the English language. He'd heard of swooping *down* – it was in fact one of his own regular hunting manoeuvres, but swooping *up* – surely a linguistic error! Should he correct young Kingfisher or should he pretend he hadn't heard it and let it go? Falling educational standards – they were undoubtedly the root cause. Just the same with humans, apparently. That's what he'd been told, at least. It was a topic he'd often discussed with Mrs Owl and one that gave him many a sleepless day. What would become of the bird community of England if they couldn't even communicate in good, grammatical English? Sloppy use of language was something that, as a human might say, really got his goat. He'd have to mention it, otherwise Kingfisher would persist in deviating from acceptable norms. And where would that lead to? Goodness only knows! Why, she'd probably start peppering her speech with slang and the like! And…and…and maybe even swear words! Where indeed would it end? Owl took a deep breath by way of preparation to point out the mistake to the little bird, but she pre-empted him by repeating her question with perhaps a hint of impatience in her piping, which seemed a little higher in pitch than normal.

'Owl, are you ready?'

'Ready when you are,' said Owl, forgetting all about linguistic niceties. He took another deep breath and girded his plumes for take-off.

They left the branch, which oscillated as Owl's weight disappeared with his departing body, and within seconds they were speeding along, just above the ripples and eddies of the water, Owl playing a rather tubby greyhound to Kingfisher's slender hare. It was a sight to behold, and it was indeed beheld, as predicted, by a heron and a cormorant. The cormorant, never a demonstrative bird, sat, impassive on a mooring post by the river bank. He must have been out fishing because his sodden wings were hanging out to dry in the breeze. On land he might have been mistaken for some kind of scarecrow but, perched above the water he looked for all the world like a tattered old umbrella blown inside out and abandoned to the elements. What, if anything, was going through his mind was anyone's guess. The heron didn't wait to see where the incongruous chase of a kingfisher by an owl would end, deciding that her first duty was to report what she had seen to anyone who would listen. Unfortunately, she could find no-one to tell, so she made for the woods and hung around in the air in her inimitable manner, to all appearances desultory, yet deceptively purposeful on this occasion, until she spotted a wood pigeon sitting on a branch cooing away, irritatingly and endlessly, to nobody in particular. The heron descended in spiral turns until a safe landing was possible on the ground just below the cooing pigeon. The story of an owl chasing a kingfisher in broad daylight and at breakneck speed along the river was duly reported to the pigeon, who said he would pass it on to the newspaper with all haste. The heron flew off, the pigeon delivered the message, and the next morning "The Woodland Bugle's" headline ran as follows:

"ANGRY OWLS STRIKE BACK". The gist of the story was that after humiliating attacks by kingfishers on owls in recent days (or rather, nights) the larger birds had regrouped and were now counter-attacking in order to take revenge and reassert themselves. Interviews with owls were promised in later editions and, if any kingfishers could be located, they would be invited to put their side of the case. The editorial was entitled "Avian anarchy – first the war of the woods and now the war of the waters". Chief Editor Fox speculated that this could be the end of civilisation as birds knew it. Were birds heading for the kind of chaos and mutual destruction that had characterised so much of human society over the centuries, and would there be a contagion, with this reckless bird behaviour spreading, domino fashion, to four-legged creatures in the woods and forests of England? The editorial ended by stating that animals and birds were living in dangerous times. Would common sense prevail? "The Woodland Bugle" was sounding a clarion call, which must be heeded.

Chapter Four

In time, things got back to normal. There were no more sightings of small birds hunting big birds or of night birds behaving like day birds. As expected, "The Woodland Bugle" didn't say sorry – in fact, didn't even consider saying sorry for its contribution to the creation of an atmosphere of near hysteria in the neighbourhood, with its exaggerated stories about bird misbehaviour, and its sensational warnings of impending doom. All this was quietly allowed to fade from the collective consciousness, and within days the paper had reverted to its traditional pattern of informing its readers about human activity: the cutting down of trees here, the dumping of rubbish there, the nuisance factor everywhere. As for Owl and Kingfisher, they declined invitations to comment on the original newspaper reports regarding their aberrant conduct, considering the whole thing a storm in a birdbath and unworthy of further discussion. They calculated that silence on the matter would expedite its journey towards oblivion, and so it did. The whole thing soon became a mere speck in fauna memory (flora didn't seem to have memory at all) and regular life resumed in the wood and in the surrounding area.

March was a windy month and April was also living up to its reputation. It was a new day and Owl had fallen asleep on his favourite branch. Rain pattering on the leaves had acted like a soothing lullaby for the hunter, weary after the exertions of the night.

'Lullabies are for babies!' Owl would have protested, with a grumpy face and a dismissive tone, if he'd heard such a description, but he didn't hear it and he did look as peaceful as a baby, slumbering, protected from the shower by several sturdy branches above where he was perched. He had no idea how long he slept but gradually, very gradually, he became aware of a distant call, repeated at regular intervals.

'Cuckoo…cuckoo…cuckoo.'

Owl remembered the conversation with his friends in December and resolved to alert them to the fact that the cuckoos were back, so that they could arrange to meet up with the summer visitors and ask them a few questions about their travels and about their child-rearing policies. Without further ado, and temporarily forgetting all about his traditional reluctance to move around in daylight, he visited Rook in his rookery, Blackbird in his hawthorn tree and Kingfisher outside her burrow on the river bank. Owl didn't normally show any interest whatsoever in the property market, but he couldn't help but make comparisons between the accommodation choices of his three friends. For a start, he wondered how anyone could maintain their sanity living in a place like the rookery. The noise was unremitting and overpowering and there was a constant toing and froing by Rook's relatives and friends. The cacophony and the frenzied activity would have driven Owl to distraction if he'd had to live there even for one day. He'd been told that in large cities railway stations used by humans were similar sorts of places, especially in what was apparently known as "the rush hour".

Rook's nesting area sounded appalling, and as soon as he had finished his conversation with his friend, Owl dived into the air and made his escape from the seething, raucous, black-feathered colony which was "The Rookery".

On his way to the hawthorn, Owl had to pass the bushes where Blackbird had lived last year. The new residents, the sparrows, were twittering away in their typical fashion, gossiping and exchanging trivial snippets of information that would be of interest to nobody but sparrows. They were the superstars of small-talk, the fraternity of frivolity and Owl was only too pleased to swish by without more than a passing glance. He decided there and then that he would congratulate Blackbird on his partner's decision to relocate to more salubrious surroundings.

The hawthorn did, indeed, prove to be a most desirable habitation – for a family of blackbirds, at least. The view over the meadows and across the river valley to the distant hills was, as an estate agent would have put it, "magnificent", or, as you or I might have put it, "very pleasing", and there was a tranquil air to the place which Owl found most appealing. Blackbird and his partner were gratified to hear Owl's heartfelt approval of their decision to vacate their former lodgings. The mere thought of the sparrows caused Blackbird to ruffle up his feathers, as if to shake off any association, however tenuous, with the unsavoury little twitterers. It would have been clear to anyone that Owl and Blackbird shared certain values, among which a consideration of themselves as being a cut above the sparrows was most definitely one.

'Well, must be going,' said Owl after a while. 'I'll let you know whether the day we've agreed on will suit Kingfisher, and then we can make contact with the cuckoos, all being well.'

'Thank you, Owl,' sang Blackbird, who was very keen to learn about Africa from the much-travelled cuckoos, and was also curious to find out more about their unusual family arrangements.

Owl flew off and was soon perched alongside Kingfisher, by the river.

'Rook, Blackbird and I are all able to meet up the day after tomorrow,' said Owl, hoping and expecting that Kingfisher would fall in with their plans.

'What time were you thinking of?' piped Kingfisher, looking slightly embarrassed, it seemed to Owl.

'Well, we thought early afternoon, just after lunch, would be a good time,' he said, that having been agreed with the other two.

'Oh dear,' piped Kingfisher. 'I'm afraid I can't manage that. I have an appointment at that time.'

'An appointment?' said Owl, wondering what kind of appointment could possibly be of sufficient importance to override a meeting with himself and his two esteemed colleagues. 'An appointment?' he repeated, sounding slightly irritated this time.

'Well, not so much an appointment,' piped Kingfisher, fidgeting on the perch and turning her face away from Owl's sharp gaze. 'It's more of a date, I suppose you could say.'

'Oh really!' said Owl, definitely irritated by this point. 'A date! An assignation! Well, surely you can postpone your date in order to fit in with the rest of us. An assignation can take place any time, after all.'

'Oh dear! This is most difficult. It really is,' piped Kingfisher who, to Owl's astonishment, proceeded to preen herself as if in preparation for some waterside beauty contest.

'Now listen,' said Owl, whose annoyance had by now developed into something more akin to outrage. (*How dare this little creature offend me by preening herself in my presence,* he thought.) His eyes were now so big that they seemed to fill the whole of his angry face. 'Listen to me. I can't possibly go back to Blackbird and Rook and tell them that you can't come at the time which suits the three of us because you have a...a...a date! They would be as offended as I am. And please stop preening yourself when I'm talking to you!'

Kingfisher looked startled at Owl's words and at the fierceness of his face.

'Oh, I'm so sorry, Owl,' she piped. 'I didn't mean to be disrespectful. Please forgive me. I really didn't wish to cause offence.' She looked completely crestfallen, and even Owl found himself softening, so vulnerable and delicate did she seem. *If birds could shed tears,* he thought, *that's probably what she'd be doing at this very moment.*

'No, no. Forgive *me,*' he said. 'I've overreacted and I normally pride myself on not losing my temper, especially when dealing with members of the opposite...er...er...er sex. So, Kingfisher, dear Kingfisher, it's for you to forgive me and not the contrary.'

Now it was Kingfisher's turn to feel the more ashamed of the two of them. She had, without intending it, brought Owl, who was, after all, old enough to be her father, to a state of contrition.

'I behaved badly,' she piped, 'and I realise now that preening myself in front of you was quite out of order, so can we pretend that none of this happened and can we be friends again, like we were before? Please?' She piped with such silkiness and her femininity was so total that Owl had no choice but to accede to her request.

'Of course we are friends, and if you have an assignation you must keep it,' he said. 'I had no right to interfere or pass judgment on your private affairs, and it's for you to give me a day when you are available and we'll see if we can fit in with you.'

'Oh, Owl! You are so sweet,' piped Kingfisher. 'I'll tell you what. I'll talk to my friend and explain that I have important business with three of my oldest and best buddies, so it'll be up to him to find another time for our date.' She looked directly into Owl's enormous face and stopped him from protesting by raising her long slim beak in such an imperious manner that he realised her word on the topic was final.

'If you say so,' he said.

'I most certainly do say so,' she piped. And that was that!

They chatted for a while about the weather and other inconsequential matters, then Owl flew back home, pleased that he and Kingfisher were still friends, and looking forward to meeting the cuckoos in just a couple of days.

The four friends met up at the spot where they held their December meetings and it was a fine day. The morning had been true to the form of an April morning with a couple of short-lived showers, and the afternoon was starting with lovely sunshine, warm to the feathers and showing off the woods at their springtime best. On every tree the leaves, still wet from the rain, glistened in the sunlight and quivered as the gentlest of breezes kissed them, brushing past on its aimless little meanderings through the wood.

'Time to look for cuckoos,' croaked Rook, anxious to get started on their mission.

'Er, may I suggest that we stay here for a short while and just listen,' said Owl, remembering that it was through his ears that he'd first become conscious of the travellers' return to the area.

'I think I know where they usually hang out,' piped Kingfisher, who was a restless little bird, unaccustomed to sitting still for more than a few minutes unless she was watching a fish and planning her hunting strategy.

'Why don't we follow Kingfisher to where she thinks they'll be and then sit and listen there for a few minutes?' sang Blackbird, considering that a compromise might keep everyone more or less content.

Rook appeared to be nodding in agreement. Owl looked far from content, but shrugged somewhere in the vicinity of his shoulders, blinked a characteristically enigmatic blink, and after a long pause went along with the majority view that they should begin their quest without further delay.

'Let Kingfisher lead the way,' said Owl in a voice designed to create the impression that the proposal had been his all along.

Kingfisher shot off in the direction of a spinney on the other side of the river. Blackbird was second off the mark, followed by Rook, whose flying technique was, to say the least, untidy, when compared with the smooth, efficient styles of the smaller birds. Owl brought up the rear, keeping his eyes sharply focused on the tail feathers of Kingfisher and

Blackbird. Rook's tendency to rise and dip and zigzag was more than Owl could cope with, so he left Rook to his own devices, knowing that he'd find his way in his own eccentric manner. And sure enough, they all ended up on the same branch of the same tree in the spinney which Kingfisher had identified as good cuckoo-hunting territory. They sat in silence, getting their breath back and waiting and hoping to hear the unmistakable call of a cuckoo. But no such call was forthcoming. They continued to wait, long after regaining their breath, and even Owl, who was normally capable of sitting quite still for hours at a time, began to look around with an air of slight impatience. Rook, sensing that Owl was ill at ease, sidled up to him and uttered a rather confidential sort of croak, just loud enough for Owl to hear, but too quiet for the smaller birds:

'I wonder if Kingfisher has brought us on a wild-cuckoo chase, if you'll pardon the expression,' he croaked, with a naughty little glint in his eye.

Owl nodded an almost imperceptible nod but thought it prudent to refrain from comment. They remained quietly at their post for at least another twenty minutes. If a human, armed with binoculars or a telescope, had seen them he would have questioned the very evidence of his own eyes for they were, indeed, a most incongruous quartet, perched like budgies in a cage, arranged in ascending order of size, Kingfisher at one end of the branch, Rook at the other.

Blackbird was on the point of suggesting they put off the cuckoo hunt for another day when, to their surprise and delight, they heard the very call they were waiting for.

'Cuckoo…Cuckoo.'

Unfortunately, it was nowhere near the spinney where they were perched. It was coming from the very wood where Blackbird, Owl and Rook had their homes – from the place where they'd met up earlier in the afternoon. Kingfisher looked as deflated as a small bird can without disappearing altogether. She stammered a rather pathetic "sorry", but the others told her not to be silly.

'Cuckoos are an unpredictable species,' croaked Rook, reassuringly. 'Very difficult to pin down, a cuckoo,' he went on. 'I remember once, some years ago, when there were far more of them around than…'

'Shh…' said Owl. 'Let's just wait here a few more minutes to be sure they're still in the same place, and then we'll make our way back to the wood and see if we can find them.'

They waited until they'd heard a few more calls, then flew back to their own wood, settling in an oak tree about halfway between Blackbird's new hawthorn dwelling and the rookery.

'Cuckoo…Cuckoo.' The call was quite close.

'It's in that beech tree over there,' sang Blackbird. 'Let's get a little nearer if we can.'

One at a time the four friends flew over to a nearby tree, from where they could clearly see the cuckoo, and it seemed that the cuckoo hadn't spotted them.

'Look,' sang Blackbird, pianissimo, so that the cuckoo wouldn't hear. 'It's got a ring on its leg.'

'Good Heavens!' croaked Rook, sotto voce. 'Humans wear rings on their fingers to show they're married. It must have gone native!'

Owl, whose eyesight was the best out of the four of them, whispered something to Rook, who croaked sotto voce to

Blackbird, who sang pianissimo to Kingfisher, who gasped in disbelief. The message, which had passed in such hushed tones from each bird to the next, was truly startling. It was that this cuckoo was not just wearing a ring but it also had something attached to its back – something that looked very much like a miniature television screen, and a tiny aerial!

'Not only has it gone native,' croaked Rook, 'it must be a spy – some kind of secret agent working for the humans.' His beak hung open, aghast at what Owl had revealed about the mysterious cuckoo. Blackbird's beautiful yellow beak was also wide open and Kingfisher was shaking her blue-capped head from side to side. They sat, dumbfounded, waiting for the cuckoo to make its call again. When it did, they quickly agreed on their next move. Kingfisher, as the smallest and least threatening in appearance, would fly across to where the cuckoo was perched and engage it in conversation, explaining that she had three friends with her and that they would all like to welcome the cuckoo to their wood and have a little chat about things.

Kingfisher waited for a couple more calls by the cuckoo, then darted across to the tree which the visitor was using as its broadcasting station.

'Good afternoon, Cuckoo,' she piped in the most dulcet tone she could manage. 'Welcome to our wood.'

'Goodness, you quite startled me,' said the cuckoo, twisting its neck to get a better view of Kingfisher, who had deliberately settled on a lower branch, to avoid appearing confrontational. 'Well thank you very much for the welcome,' the cuckoo went on. 'To be honest, I'm rather surprised that this *is* your wood. I thought kingfishers always nested next to water.'

'I see you're very well-informed,' piped Kingfisher. 'You're quite right. I don't actually live in the wood, but some of my best friends do and, as it happens, they're sitting in that tree over there and would love to be introduced to you. May I invite them over?'

'By all means. Oh, er, how many are there?' asked the cuckoo, sounding just a little wary and wondering if kingfishers were birds one could entirely trust.

'There are three of them – a blackbird, a rook and an owl,' piped Kingfisher, hoping that the mention of Rook and Owl would not sound too intimidating to the cuckoo, since Rook, in particular, was quite a large bird and Owl was, after all, a bird of prey.

'I think I'd prefer to meet them one at a time, if you don't mind,' said the cuckoo, knowing that *Cuculus canorus,* to use the Latin title, came with a certain amount of baggage and that other birds were sometimes resentful and could even be hostile. "Best to be cautious" was a phrase beloved of cuckoos. 'I'll tell you what, why don't you hop up here onto my branch, and then you could invite your friend the blackbird to come and perch where you are at the moment?'

Kingfisher was usually rather good at thinking on her feet but felt quite flustered by the cuckoo's obvious reluctance to meet all four of them at the same time. After a moment's hesitation, she tried again.

'I believe it *was* actually Blackbird who originally mentioned that he would like to meet a cuckoo to find out about Africa,' she piped, 'but I know that Owl, who is quite old and very wise, would also like to hear all about your travels, so I would love him to be present when you're recounting your experiences.' Kingfisher looked up at the

49

cuckoo to see if there was any reaction, for she was using her most appealing intonation, and combining it with the sort of body language which usually brought her success at the riverside, so she was optimistic that she would be able to get round the newcomer.

'Well, alright,' said the cuckoo. 'Just the blackbird and the owl. But nobody else.'

'Ah well, that's a bit of a problem,' piped Kingfisher, who was warming to her task and beginning to sense victory. 'You see, Owl and Rook are old mates and behave like a couple of very close brothers. They go everywhere and do everything together,' she fibbed, 'and they are both so gentle that I'm sure you'd be delighted by their friendliness and their courteous ways. I myself spend lots of time with them and they really are excellent company, though, between you and me, they are a bit set in their ways, what humans call "conservative", (that's with just a small "c", of course) if you know what I mean.'

'I know exactly what you mean,' said the cuckoo, 'and you really are twisting my wing, aren't you?' Kingfisher was heartened to spot a knowing wink in the cuckoo's eye. 'Alright then, I give in,' said the larger bird, 'but I insist that you come up here and sit by my side so that your friends can perch together on the lower branch.'

'No problem at all,' piped Kingfisher, feeling quite proud at seeing her powers of persuasion so amply and promptly rewarded. She spread her elegant little wings and fluttered up to where the cuckoo was perched. For the first time, she had an opportunity to catch a glimpse of the cuckoo's body and, sure enough, there was some sort of apparatus attached to its shoulder. The temptation was to look again, properly, but in spite of what others sometimes said about her, Kingfisher was, in most respects, a well-brought-up bird, and her mother had taught her among other things that it was impolite and improper to stare at others, especially if they were disabled or different in some way.

'So it's alright if I call them over?' Kingfisher piped, anxious to get her friends into conversation with the unconventional stranger.

'As you wish,' replied the cuckoo. And in the time it would take a cuckoo to say "cuckoo" a couple of times, Kingfisher had called to her waiting friends and they were already in the air and preparing to land on the cuckoo's tree.

'On the lower branch, if you don't mind,' called the cuckoo, making it abundantly clear that cuckoo rules applied in that particular tree.

Blackbird came first, settling without fuss on the bough vacated by Kingfisher. Owl came next and Rook joined the two of them with a good deal of flapping and fluttering, which he seemed to need in order to achieve balance. This landing by Rook was a most inelegant spectacle, which the cuckoo watched with a mixture of wry amusement and a tiny pinch of alarm, but once Rook had settled himself the cuckoo seemed reassured and waited for the newcomers to introduce themselves. However, it was Kingfisher who piped up, choosing to make the introductions herself.

'May I present my three best friends,' she piped, 'Blackbird on the left, Owl in the middle and Rook...'

'On the right,' interjected the cuckoo drily. 'It's certainly true that I regularly fly to places where birds are exotically clad, but I can still tell the difference between a good old English Rook, an English Owl and a Blackbird.' This was uttered in the sort of confident tone one often encounters in the widely travelled. It bordered on the supercilious.

Rook felt sorry for Kingfisher, who looked hurt by the cuckoo's put-down. He considered making a barbed riposte to put the cuckoo in its place, but decided to hold his tongue in the interests of harmony and good relations with the summer visitor, or "immigrant", as Owl might have described the newcomer. It was, in fact, Owl who spoke next.

'My friends and I, established residents of this area, would like to take the opportunity of welcoming you to our wood,' he said, ponderous as ever.

'Thanks indeed,' replied the cuckoo. 'As you probably know I'm only here for a short while and then I'll be away on my travels again. That's the way it is with us cuckoos, but it's good to know I'm welcome while I'm here.'

'Indeed, you are,' croaked Rook, 'and I suppose you may be wondering why we've made a point of approaching you in this way after years of ignoring your regular visits to our little patch?'

'It had crossed my mind,' said the cuckoo, 'but I meet all sorts when I travel, so nothing surprises me anymore. But go ahead, by all means, tell me the worst.'

Rook was beginning to be irritated by the cockiness and seeming lack of respect in the cuckoo's way of speaking but, as outsiders, maybe cuckoos didn't know any better.

'Well, the thing is, our friend Blackbird here would love to know about your journeys to Africa, and Owl is interested in your family arrangements.'

'Family arrangements! What do you mean "family arrangements"?' said the cuckoo, sounding quite indignant, and fluffing up its feathers to make itself look bigger.

'Perhaps I should explain,' said Owl, whose interest in cuckoo child policy was no greater than that of his friends, but since Rook had singled him out, he felt an obligation to speak.

'I think you *should* explain,' said the cuckoo, 'but before you do are you sure there aren't any other matters, personal or otherwise, that you'd like to quiz me about?' The cuckoo's tone was clearly sarcastic and, as such, was not intended to encourage further questions, intrusive or otherwise. Rook, however, either failed to detect the annoyance and sarcasm in the cuckoo's voice or deliberately chose to ignore them, for he came straight out with the very question they were all dying to ask but hadn't dared.

'Yes, I have a question,' he croaked. 'In fact, I have two.' The cuckoo looked in astonishment at Rook, wondering whether the large bird sitting just below him was being deliberately provocative, or was too stupid to recognize irony when he heard it.

Rook pressed on. 'Well, to come straight to the point, we've noticed that you're wearing jewellery, and you also seem to be carrying a TV around with you, complete with aerial. What's all that about, if you don't mind me asking? Is it for your new family to watch when they leave their nests?' Rook pointedly used the plural, since each cuckoo egg was known to be laid in a different nest.

Before the cuckoo had a chance to react, Rook threw in another question, just for good measure: 'And we were also wondering whether you're a male or a female cuckoo?'

The cuckoo started to laugh, in a "cuckooish" sort of way. The irritation seemed to have dissipated just as quickly as it had appeared and Rook's final question was answered without delay.

'I'm a male cuckoo and I'm surprised you didn't know. We males are the famous ones. We're the ones who call: "Cuckoo." Our mates, the females, make a babbling sound. Totally different, but sweet in its own way. At least, *we* think so.'

'Well, that's cleared that one up at least,' croaked Rook. 'Now, what about the others...the jewellery and the TV?'

The cuckoo laughed again, then leaned out from his branch and peered down, looking directly into Rook's eye. 'I presume when you say "jewellery" you're referring to the ring on my leg?'

Rook nodded.

'Ah well, that's been put there by a very important subspecies of human known as ornithologists. They consider cuckoos to be of great interest, so they've ringed me for purposes of identification. It's not jewellery, it's an identity tag.' The cuckoo raised his leg to show off the ring, which certainly impressed Kingfisher, who was wishing that ornithologists would find *kingfishers* of great interest so that she, too, could have such a fine trinket attached to *her* leg.

All four local birds were fascinated by what the cuckoo was telling them and they wanted to know more.

'And the TV?' croaked Rook, by way of a prompt.

The cuckoo didn't reply immediately. It was as if he wanted to keep his audience in suspense, knowing that when he did speak the dramatic effect would be all the greater.

'Well, dear friends,' he started. 'What you see on my back is not a television set. No, no, no! Nothing so prosaic! What you see there is the very latest technology – human technology, that is. It's state of the art. It's hi-tech, it's...'

'I'm sure it's all those things, but what *is* it?' interrupted Rook, who couldn't contain his impatience.

The cuckoo was beginning to enjoy being the centre of attention and he also liked the feeling of power it gave him. He knew that rooks, being members of the crow family, had a reputation for cleverness, so it gave him particular pleasure to be able to tease a real live rook, to play with him like a cat with a mouse. He stood as high on his legs as he could and he puffed out his chest as if to say, 'Look at me. Look how important I am, and listen carefully to what I'm about to tell you because you'll never have heard anything quite like it before.'

'Tell us. What is it you've got on your back?' Now it was Owl's voice urging the cuckoo to come to the point.

'I'll tell you,' said the cuckoo. 'What I have on my back has been there for the last two years and it's been with me to Africa. Twice. It's travelled twenty thousand miles on my back, and it'll be returning to Africa again once I've performed my paternal duties here in this English wood. What you thought was a miniature television screen is, in fact, a solar panel.'

'A solar panel!' croaked Rook.

'Indeed, a solar panel,' said the cuckoo, 'and I think I can guess what you're thinking. You rooks are smart birds, so they tell me, and I imagine you're putting two and two together and coming up with some incredible theory or other. It wouldn't surprise me if you've come to the conclusion that I'm some sort of bionic bird, using solar power to get me to Africa and back without needing to flap my wings or use up the food-stock in my body. Is that what you're thinking, Mr Rook?'

'I really don't know what to think,' said Rook, who was, by now, feeling most frustrated at being kept on tenterhooks by the enigmatic cuckoo.

'What's the solar panel for?' sang Blackbird, hoping that his musical contribution might tempt the cuckoo to reveal the secret they all wanted so much to hear.

'The solar panel is there to charge and recharge a tiny battery, which is also on my back, and the whole apparatus is none other than a satellite-tracking device, attached to my body by the human subspecies I mentioned before – the ornithologists. What do you think of that?' The cuckoo puffed out his chest even more, until it looked as if it might burst. He sounded boastful, triumphal, arrogant even. But what he was saying had captivated his audience and they sat still, trying to take in the meaning of what they'd heard.

'What you've told us is most interesting – intriguing,' said Owl after a pause. 'But I think I speak for us all if I ask you to explain what all this is about. Why have the ornithologists fixed this tracking thing to your back, and isn't it heavy to fly with and doesn't it hurt you in any way? Please do tell us more.'

'Well, it's like this,' said the cuckoo. 'The ornithologists study birds. That's what they do.'

'We know that. We know that,' croaked Rook, growing increasingly impatient. If there was one thing he disliked it was being patronised, especially by a bird which was, to all intents and purposes, a guest in his wood.

'I didn't know that,' piped Kingfisher. 'Why are they called ornithologists? Why aren't they called "birdists" if they study birds?'

'Don't ask me,' said the cuckoo. 'All I know is they're called ornithologists and they always have been.'

'Er, I believe it comes from the Greek,' said Owl, who didn't really know, but thought it a pretty safe bet.

'Oh, thank you Owl,' piped Kingfisher. 'You really are such a very wise bird. Everyone says so.'

'Can we get back to the point,' croaked Rook. 'Tell us about this tracking device and what it does.'

'Well, as I was trying to say, the ornithologists, here in England, have been studying cuckoos for quite a long time and they've found out that our numbers have declined by more than fifty per cent in the last ten years,' said the cuckoo. He paused. 'They're worried about us because we're so important,' he continued, 'so they're using the satellite tracking device to find out more about our way of life, where we go in winter and so on. If they can find out why our numbers are going down, they might be able to help us to build up again. That's it in a nutshell,' he said.

'Why are cuckoos so important?' piped Kingfisher into Owl's ear.

'Shhh…' said Owl.

'I heard that,' said the cuckoo. 'I'll tell you why we're important. It's because we're unique. We're the only birds who…'

'Lay their eggs in other birds' nests,' croaked Rook.

'That's not what I was going to say,' said the cuckoo, 'but if that's what you want to discuss, then we'll discuss it.'

'Well, could we discuss your tracking device first?' croaked Rook, who really wanted to get to the bottom of the mystery.

'As you wish,' said the cuckoo. 'If you want all the details, you shall have all the details. Are you ready?'

'We are,' came the response from all four birds.

'So, here goes: it weighs five grams and it transmits for ten hours at a time. After that, it goes into "sleep mode" for forty-eight hours, and that allows the solar panel to recharge the battery.'

'And do all cuckoos wear them?' piped Kingfisher.

The cuckoo laughed. 'No, no, no. Only four of us. We were specially chosen,' he said proudly.

'How were you specially chosen?' croaked Rook, beginning to get a little suspicious.

'Er, well, er, the ornithologists chose us… *especially*,' said the cuckoo, who suddenly looked and sounded rather less confident than before.

'But *how* were you specially chosen?' insisted Rook who, had he been a human, would probably have been a detective or a barrister.

'Well if you must know, I was trapped in a net, and the ornithologists ringed my leg and attached the tracker to my back. Satisfied?'

The four listeners looked at each other, then nodded to the cuckoo. Yes, for the moment they appeared to be satisfied.

Chapter Five

'Now, if you'll excuse me, I have a number of things to attend to,' said the cuckoo, in a tone that discouraged any kind of appeal. It had such a ring of finality about it that Owl and his friends accepted it for what it was: a rather unceremonious "goodbye".

'There are still a few things we'd love to discuss with you,' croaked Rook, 'so we'll pop up here another time to carry on our conversation, if that's alright with you?'

'Perfectly alright, as long as I'm free,' said the cuckoo, hinting at a life heavy with commitments.

The four friends flew off in the direction of their wood, but when Kingfisher invited them to stop by at the river the three larger birds were more than happy to accept because they all felt that there were things to be talked about. There was unfinished business and an exchange of views was required.

'Well, what did you make of that?' sang Blackbird once they'd all settled on a willow branch overhanging the river.

'It begs more questions than it answers,' croaked Rook. 'Interesting birds, cuckoos,' he went on, 'but I wouldn't trust them further than I could see them, or hear them, for that matter.'

'I liked the ring on his leg,' piped Kingfisher, 'and the pattern of bands around his chest was delightful, though I must say I prefer my turquoise colouring to his rather drab blue-grey.'

'Be that as it may,' said Owl, 'we still don't know anything about the travels in Africa and we didn't get an opportunity to question him about his family life – in particular, the egg distribution business.'

'Quite so,' croaked Rook. 'And I think there's a lot more to that tracking device than meets the eye. I don't think we've heard the half of it, to tell you the truth.'

'So what shall we do, what shall we do?' sang Blackbird in a melody that was more plaintive than interrogative.

'Well before anything else we need to fix a time to go back and question the cuckoo further,' said Owl, turning his head first to the left, where Blackbird was perched, and then to the right, where Kingfisher and Rook were sitting, the one resplendent in her colourful attire, the other cassock-black like a priest.

'How about the day after tomorrow, at the same time?' sang Blackbird. 'That gives him time to do the things he needs to do, and we don't have to wait too long to find out what we want to know.'

'Fine with me,' piped Kingfisher.

'Me, too,' croaked Rook.

'The day after tomorrow it is,' said Owl. 'Now, is there anything else we need to deal with while we're all here together?'

'Well,' croaked Rook. 'This business with the cuckoo and the ornithologists – this satellite tracking thing he's carrying around with him has got me thinking about the relationship we all have with humans. I mean, they seem to be in control of a lot of things that actually affect us, and I'm not too happy about it.'

'What do you have in mind?' said Owl, a quizzical look taking over his tawny face.

'Well for a start there's the matter of hedges. I know it's the humans who planted most of them in the first place, but they've pulled up so many that there are only half the number there were twenty years ago. There used to be half a million miles, and now it's a quarter of a million! That's had a devastating effect on some of those birds that used them for nesting. And then there are the pesticides. They kill off so many insects that there isn't enough food for some of our cousin birds. And there's the pollution! What couldn't I say about pollution! The problem is I wouldn't know where to begin!'

'You're right, Rook. I know you're right,' said Owl, 'but what can we do? It seems to me that we're powerless. And it's not only in England, you know. And it's not just a recent thing, either. I was told by a friend that in China, sixty or seventy years ago, they had a policy of killing as many birds as they could because the birds were eating seeds that were needed to grow crops for the human population. And guess what happened? When they'd killed most of the birds they had a plague of insects, because there were no birds to eat the flies and all the other little bugs!'

'Well I've heard that story, too,' croaked Rook. 'And did you know that at the same time people in China were not allowed to own dogs... not in the cities, anyway? The only dog in Beijing, or Peking as we called it then, was an Afghan hound, and that belonged to the Swiss Ambassador. You'd think that at the very least he'd have had the courtesy to own a Pekinese, wouldn't you!'

'Well I never!' said Owl. 'It makes you think. It really does. They have so much power, the humans, and yet they exercise it in some very strange ways.'

'Could I say something?' sang Blackbird. 'I don't think all the humans are bad. I've got a relative who lives in the suburbs and when he's in people's gardens he can sometimes hear voices from televisions in the houses. And he told me that there are two brothers named David and Jonathan Something and David does programmes about birds and animals and all sorts of living things and that he's a very good man because he loves nature.'

'Er, I believe you're thinking of two brothers named David and Richard, not David and Jonathan,' croaked Rook. 'David and Jonathan are both political pundits. No connection with wildlife, I think you'll find.'

'What are political pundits?' piped Kingfisher, who was beginning to feel quite lost.

'Well,' croaked Rook, 'there are politicians and political pundits. Together they're another sort of human subspecies.'

'Oh,' piped Kingfisher. 'So are the politicians the adults, like pigs, and the pundits are like piglets?' she asked.

'Er no,' croaked Rook, who was trying hard to think of a good way to explain it all to Kingfisher.

'Politicians talk about politics to other politicians,' said Owl.

'And the pundits talk about politics to all the other humans,' croaked Rook. 'That's the main difference, but in England, the politicians have this thing called Prime Minister's Questions, and the rule is that when one politician is talking the others have to keep interrupting by making animal noises. It's a peculiar sort of ritual they perform on a regular basis.'

'What kind of animal noises?' piped Kingfisher, puzzled that humans should behave in such an odd way.

'Oh, braying donkey noises, mostly,' croaked Rook, but they have a number of variations which they use according to the mood they're in.'

'Er, I think we're straying from the subject,' said Owl, who was sometimes prone to a little digression of his own, but disapproved of it in others.

'Well, I'd just like to repeat what I said earlier,' sang Blackbird. 'David Thingamajig – the one with a brother named Richard (who's dead now, anyway), does these wonderful television programmes which make other humans appreciate nature and think about the future of the planet, so they're not all bad and they're not all against us.'

'Thank you, Blackbird,' said Owl. 'I think you've made your point very well, but it still remains the case that humans cause us many problems, and it's only right that we should discuss the implications and consider our situation.'

'If I may, I'd like to personalise the discussion,' croaked Rook, who seemed to have his own agenda and was determined to air his views while he had a ready-made audience, and one which was likely to be sympathetic to what he said.

'By all means,' said Owl. 'Please do go ahead.'

'Well, as I'm sure you know, my Latin name is Corvus frugilegus, which simply means "food-gathering crow". Now, not so very long ago farmers in England were under the impression that we, the rooks, were destroying the crops they planted because they saw us feeding in the fields and disturbing the young plants. It's true that sometimes the plants died, but most of them survived, and what the farmers didn't know was that they survived because of us.'

'That sounds a bit odd,' sang Blackbird. 'Why did they survive after you and your friends had disturbed them and how can you take the credit?'

'Good questions,' croaked Rook, 'and I just wish the farmers had taken the trouble to find out the answers to those very questions, because what they did instead was kill us. They killed as many of us as they could, and the rook population dropped dramatically as a result. It took those stupid humans years and years to realise that our feeding habits were more beneficial than harmful to their crops, because we were disturbing the plants in order to eat the leatherjackets and wireworms that were feeding on the roots. If we hadn't eaten the worms, the worms would have killed the crops. End of story!'

'Goodness!' said Owl. 'I never knew that.'

'Nor me,' sang Blackbird.

'What's a leatherjacket?' piped Kingfisher.

'The leatherjacket is the larva of the daddy longlegs, and the wireworm is the larva of the click beetle, and both of them live under the soil and eat the roots of plants, so they're pests,' croaked Rook with all the vehemence of an aggrieved bird. 'But those ignorant farmers thought *we* were the pests – the rooks. Now they know better and they leave us alone because they realise that we help more than we hinder.'

'That's a fascinating and, of course, disturbing story,' said Owl. 'Does anyone else wish to say anything, on similar lines or indeed on different lines?'

Blackbird said that in his opinion the picture was a mixed one.

'It's certainly true that humans have done bad things in the past,' he sang, 'but some of them do lots of good things now. For example, the suburban blackbirds and all the other so-called garden birds are often provided with birdbaths, bird tables and daily rations of food.'

'Ah yes, but is it the right kind of food?' asked Rook. 'Are white bread and pizza crusts good for birds' digestive systems? Is bacon really healthy for a bird's cardio-vascular arrangements? I think not!'

'Well,' sang Blackbird, determined to stand up to Rook and his arguments, 'if it's the middle of winter and the ground is frozen solid I think a bit of bread and bacon served up on a table is better than an earthworm you can't get at.'

'And do you know what humans call that sort of situation?' croaked Rook. 'They have a little proverb which says "a bird in the hand is worth two in the bush". So what does that tell us about our friends the humans?' he croaked, hanging as much sarcasm as he possibly could on the word "friends".

'It's not the most respectful of sayings, I grant you, but Blackbird makes a fair point,' said Owl, who loved nothing better than adjudicating in debates and disagreements. He felt it gave him the gravitas that was his entitlement.

'Alright, what else have the humans done that's good for us?' asked Rook, who couldn't think of any positive things himself and thought it unlikely that Blackbird would be able to either.

'Well, I happen to know that they've re-introduced red kites and ospreys, and I heard just last week that they're reintroducing cranes to this country – and cranes haven't lived in England for four hundred years!' sang Blackbird with all the verve and vigour of a convert. 'Now I know that all those species disappeared because of what humans did to them in the past, but at least they've learned their lesson and they're doing what they can to make amends.'

'It's undeniable that some humans are trying hard to right the wrongs of history,' said Owl, who was impressed with Blackbird's grasp of the facts.

'Well all that may be true,' croaked a grudging Rook, 'but just think for a moment about some of the nonsense the humans have come up with over the years. Why, for example, do they call a colony of penguins a rookery, for goodness' sake? How bizarre is that! A rookery is obviously the home of rooks. The clue is in the name! So, the home of penguins! I ask you!'

'That is a slight anomaly,' said Owl, who had, until that moment, been unaware that penguins did live in rookeries.

'Slight!' croaked Rook in the highest pitch he could manage. 'Anomaly!' he croaked, somehow finding an even higher note. 'And then there's that insulting collective noun they use for a group of rooks…and owls, for that matter!' The indignation in his voice was matched by a fiery glint in his black, black eyes. He glared at Owl, who seemed quite nonplussed and appeared to have lost his customary composure.

'A g-group of owls…' he stammered. 'I didn't know there was a collective noun for a group of owls.'

'Well there is. And it's the same as a group of rooks,' croaked Rook.

'So what is it?' asked Kingfisher and Blackbird in unison.

66

'I can hardly bring myself to say the word,' croaked Rook. 'It's…it's…it's a "parliament of rooks", and it's a "parliament of owls", would you believe!'

'What does "parliament" mean?' piped Kingfisher.

'Another good question,' croaked Rook. 'It's that place where the politicians make their animal noises every week,' he added, spitting out the words with equal doses of venom and distaste.

'Well,' said Owl, 'I think you should be grateful for small mercies, Rook, because I happen to know the collective noun for your cousins, the crows, and I don't think you'd be too happy if it were applied to you!'

'And what would that be?' asked Rook in a tone of resignation and helplessness.

'A group of crows is known as a "murder of crows",' said Owl, looking at each bird in turn, to see what reaction this phrase had provoked.

Blackbird seemed shocked; Kingfisher looked bewildered, but Rook just rocked backwards and forwards on his big grey feet. For once it seemed that words failed him.

Owl was beginning to worry that Rook might have lots more grievances up his metaphorical sleeve, and thought the judicious course of action would be to draw the proceedings to a close before his friend became over-excited.

'Er, I think we've been given plenty of food for thought,' he said, turning towards Rook before looking at the two smaller birds. 'It might be best to leave matters there for the time being, though I'm sure we'll return to many of these things in the future. May I suggest that we meet here, outside Kingfisher's burrow, the day after tomorrow, after lunch, so that we can resume our conversation with the cuckoo and find out some of the things we failed to discover today.'

The others agreed, the three male birds bade farewell to Kingfisher, then flew up to the wood, where they went their separate ways.

Chapter Six

They met up on the appointed day, outside Kingfisher's burrow, to track down the cuckoo once again and continue their polite interrogation. The only thing was, the four birds were no longer four. They had, actually, become five! Kingfisher was there, sweet and well turned-out, as always. Blackbird was present, dapper in his black suit. Owl was just Owl. But Rook was there in duplicate...or so it seemed. He arrived with all his usual flapping and fuss, but so did another rook, almost indistinguishable from the Rook they knew. Owl, Blackbird and Kingfisher looked at each other, then focused their gaze on Rook, and waited for an explanation, which was not long in coming.

'Allow me to introduce my niece,' croaked Rook. 'This,' he added, pointing with his beak to the rook perched beside him, 'is my niece.' The pointing with the beak and the statement that the indicated bird *was* his niece seemed superfluous, in the circumstances, but that was Rook!

'Hello,' croaked the niece. 'My uncle has told me all about you and we wondered if I may join you on your little adventure to see the cuckoo.'

'I'm Blackbird,' sang Blackbird. 'Delighted to make your acquaintance.'

'And I'm Kingfisher,' piped Kingfisher, who was overjoyed at the prospect of having a fellow female in their company.

'I'm Owl,' said Owl. 'It's most certainly a pleasure to meet you, and I'm sure we'd all agree that your company would be delightful, but I must confess to a slight concern which, with your permission, I would like to discuss with your uncle and my other friends before we put our plans into action.'

The niece looked a little put out, and Rook, knowing Owl as he did, had an inkling of what was about to be said. He knew that Owl was a stickler for protocol, and would not approve of a fifth bird joining the group without prior warning and a vote of approval from all existing members. However, this was not just any bird, this was Rook's niece, and due to matters beyond Rook's control, there had been no opportunity to consult his friends in advance. He prepared to put his case before Owl could say any more.

'Dear friends,' croaked Rook. 'I fully realise that it must have surprised you when I arrived here with my niece, whose name, by the way, is Rachel. Unfortunately, circumstances prevented me from informing you beforehand, because she arrived this very morning after an absence from the rookery of three years, and since her parents are both deceased I am her guardian. After hearing her account of the last three years I felt that it would be inappropriate for me to leave her while I joined you three on the cuckoo trail. I therefore had to decide whether to absent myself from your mission or bring Rachel along with me.'

'This all sounds most interesting,' said Owl. 'I wonder if your niece would be kind enough to enlighten us regarding

70

her three years away from our wood – with your permission, of course, Rook, in your capacity as guardian and relative.' Owl turned and nodded first to Rachel and then to Rook himself.

'I have no objection whatsoever,' croaked Rook. 'In fact, I believe that my niece will be able to give you an account which will simultaneously shock and intrigue you, and as a result, I think you will have no hesitation in inviting her to accompany us on our little expedition.'

'Please proceed,' said Owl, moving his head in what one could only describe as a bow to the rather bemused niece.

'Well,' croaked Rachel. 'As my uncle said, I arrived back at the rookery unannounced in the early hours of this morning after three years away. Those three years were spent as a captive of the humans.'

There was a gasp from Blackbird and a smaller one from Kingfisher, whose lungs were, of course, slightly less capacious than those of Blackbird. Owl inflated his chest and opened his eyes as wide as they would go, which was very wide indeed. Rook just nodded like a sage. Rachel continued her story:

'Humans stole me from the nest, with three other, unrelated fledglings, and the four of us were taken far from here to a famous university where we were eventually used for research purposes.'

'That sounds horrific,' sang Blackbird.

'Awful. You poor thing! How on earth did you get through it all?' piped Kingfisher, who had always been wary of humans, keeping them at a distance by hiding her nest underground and rarely straying far from running water, for she knew that humans, in general, were not a water-based species.

'Which famous university were you at, and what was the nature of the research you were engaged in?' asked Owl, who had something of a reputation for status awareness and who was considered by some to be a bit of a snob.

'Well, since you ask, it was the University of Cambridge,' croaked Rachel, who seemed to be totally free from pretensions.

'And the research?' said Owl.

'We were allowed to fly around in an enclosure, the four of us, most of the time, but when the humans used us for research we were separated and put into cages, so that we couldn't see each other or hear each other or communicate with each other in any way. They did lots of experiments with us, but the purpose of them all was to test our intelligence.'

'Oh, I see,' said Owl, whose voice suddenly sounded less enthusiastic than it had before.

'Can you tell us about some of the experiments, please?' sang Blackbird, who had, after all, been Rook's pupil in intelligence as part of their Christmas arrangement.

'Well, there was one where I was in this cage and the human put a tall thin glass in with me. At the bottom of the glass, I could see lots of wriggling worms in a little bucket, but it was impossible for me to reach down such a tall narrow glass. The human had also left a long piece of wire in the cage. She watched to see what I'd do, knowing that I was hungry since I hadn't been fed all day.'

'So, what *did* you do?' sang Blackbird. 'Did you knock the glass over with your foot so that the worms fell out? I think that's what I would have done,' he sang, sensing that his intelligence lessons from Rook were beginning to pay off by giving him problem-solving skills that would have been denied ordinary blackbirds.

'That's brilliant!' piped Kingfisher. 'I'd never have thought of that. Well done Blackbird!'

'Um, I'm afraid that particular solution was out of the question,' croaked Rachel. 'The glass was fixed to a large wooden base, so there was no possibility of tipping it over.'

'Oh,' came a combined response from Blackbird and Kingfisher.

Owl appeared to have lost all interest in the conversation and had closed his eyes as if in a trance. Rook was looking on with all the interest that Owl seemed to have lost, boosted by a significant portion of avuncular pride.

'No, what I did was pick up the wire with my beak, put the end of it inside the top rim of the glass and push it so that it bent into the shape of a hook. Then I lowered it into the glass and used the hook to pull up the bucket of worms. Quite easy, really!'

'Bravo!' croaked Rook. 'Bravo!'

'That really is brilliant,' sang Blackbird. 'I'd never have thought of that.'

'Nor me,' piped Kingfisher, 'but to tell you the truth I don't eat worms anyway!'

They all laughed, except Owl, who opened his eyes but said nothing.

'Tell us another trick…er, sorry, experiment,' sang Blackbird.

'Alright. Just one more, for now,' croaked Rachel. 'Otherwise, the day will be gone.'

'Tell them about the stones,' croaked Rook. 'That was an interesting one, as well.'

'Well, this one's also about food and I'm sorry Kingfisher, but it's about a grub, which we rooks just love and which I'm sure you kingfishers wouldn't touch.'

'You're so right,' piped Kingfisher, 'but whenever you say grub I'll just think of a fish instead.'

Rachel laughed, then continued her story.

'Again, it was a tall glass, but this time it was a single grub and it was floating in a couple of centimetres of water at the bottom. Next to the glass, the human had left a pile of pebbles.'

'So, you broke the glass by hitting it with the pebbles,' sang Blackbird, believing he must be right this time, thanks to his private tuition from Rook.

'I'm afraid not,' croaked Rachel. 'The glass was thick and looked strong, so I never even considered trying. I'd never have been able to hit it with enough force to break it.'

'So, what *did* you do?' piped Kingfisher. 'What *could* you do?'

'What I did was drop a pebble into the glass so that the water level rose. And then another pebble to make it rise a bit more, and so on until the water and the floating grub were near the top of the glass, and then I could get the grub with my beak and, as they say in books, dinner was served!'

'Fantastic,' sang Blackbird. 'You rooks really are so very intelligent. It's a real privilege to meet a bird who's done so much for science, and at Cambridge University, too!'

'Can grubs swim?' piped Kingfisher, whose focus was not quite on the relevant part of the experiment, but who was, at

74

least, showing more interest than Owl, whose eyes had again closed quite firmly.

'I don't know whether they can swim,' croaked Rachel, 'but they can certainly float.' She laughed in a croaky, good-natured sort of way. 'The other thing is, I could see the human watching me as I performed these tasks, and I saw her smiling to herself, the way humans do. I got the impression she was going to take all the credit for what I was doing. But that's humans for you, I suppose!'

'So, what happened next?' sang Blackbird, keen to hear more of the niece's incredible adventure with the humans.

'Well, there were other experiments, which I'll tell you about another time, but all the things I did were filmed, and the same for my three fellow rooks, and now, would you believe, we're stars on the Internet!'

'I'll tell you what happened next,' croaked Rook, whose pride in his niece was obvious to all, except Owl, of course, who had retreated into stand-offish mode. 'What happened next was that the researchers at Cambridge came to the conclusion that rooks have a sophisticated intelligence to rival that of chimpanzees, because we rooks can make tools with our beaks just as chimps can craft tools with their hands. The thing is, you see, that most animals learn tricks by a process of trial and error, but the rooks in these experiments, including my beautiful niece, solved the wire problem immediately. And what's more, no other birds could have shown them how to do it since all four of them had been raised in captivity.'

'The only other thing your friends need to know,' croaked Rachel, 'is that the humans had kept records of where they'd taken us from and, now that they have all the data they want, they decided to return us to our rookery, and that's what happened this morning, after three long years in captivity. Oh, and in case you're wondering why I have a name – why I'm called Rachel, that's because of the humans. They gave all four of us names: I'm Rachel and there was Rex, Rosie and Ronald. There's nothing as pleasing to a human as a bit of alliteration, you know. Ronald the rook, Mickie the mouse, Willy the whale, they just love it. The reason they gave *us* names was so that they could tell us apart, but also because that's what humans do. They give everything a name, from donkeys on the beach to hurricanes in the sky. Daisy the donkey, Hurricane Katrina and so on.'

'That's certainly quite a story,' sang Blackbird, who was deeply impressed by the scientific achievements of Rook's niece, but was saddened that the poor bird had been taken from her family as a chick and kept as a prisoner for three years. 'What a story!' he repeated.

'And you'll never guess what one of the humans' newspapers wrote as a headline to the story of my niece,' croaked Rook, who was hopping from leg to leg in his evident excitement to reveal this final part of the story. 'The headline said: "Rook with a hook proves bird brains are the equal of monkeys." How about that!'

'I love that,' piped Kingfisher. 'Makes one proud to be a bird, doesn't it!'

'It certainly does,' croaked Rook, who was amused that Kingfisher, not exactly the brightest of birds, was taking a share of the glory. He was, of course, too fond of Kingfisher to make any comment, but he caught the eye of his niece and gave her a discreet wink. Now, as we noted before, it's virtually impossible for a bird to smile, but Rachel made a valiant attempt, rather than return her uncle's wink and risk being seen by Kingfisher, to whom she had already taken a liking and who she would hate to offend.

'Well,' said Owl, 'since circumstances have changed somewhat, I think we need to reconsider matters. I strongly suspect that if all five of us were to attempt a meeting with the cuckoo we would get a negative response, bearing in mind that Kingfisher had to use some creative stratagems and not a little wiliness to gain access for the four of us last time, so I suggest that we postpone our little expedition until tomorrow, and that Rook comes without his niece or that his niece comes without him. That must be a matter for them to decide between themselves.'

There was a silence from the other four birds, and if an adjective could have been fixed to that silence it would doubtless have been one with eleven letters, the number required to make the word "embarrassed". The silence of Blackbird, Kingfisher, Rook and Rachel was the epitome of embarrassed silence, for Owl had not attempted to exercise the diplomatic skills which many considered to be his hallmark. He had been polite when introduced to Rachel, but it was clear that all this talk of rook intelligence had touched a raw nerve, and Owl had had enough for one day.

'So be it,' croaked Rook. 'One of us will see you all tomorrow.' And with that, he took off with his niece. Owl went next, leaving Blackbird and Kingfisher alone on the branch, both of them gazing blankly into the distance. Kingfisher broke the silence.

'Owl was probably right that another bird, especially one as big as a rook, would have been a problem for the cuckoo,' she piped, 'but I think he was a bit blunt, don't you?'

'I certainly do,' sang Blackbird. 'And I'll tell you something else. I don't know whether you noticed, but as soon as he knew that Rook's niece had been taken away for the purpose of intelligence testing he appeared to lose all interest in her story.'

'Yes, now that you say it,' piped Kingfisher. 'Why do you think that was?'

'Well, if it's possible to have a chip on your shoulder when you haven't really got shoulders, that's what he's got, in my opinion,' sang Blackbird.

'I'm not sure I understand what that means,' piped Kingfisher in her usual, open manner.

'Well, as you probably know,' sang Blackbird, 'Owl is often represented wearing a cap and gown as if he had a university degree, but in truth, he's never even set foot inside a school, let alone a university. Birds can't, can they! He calls himself an autodidact, which just means that he's self-taught, and he resents the fact that he never got any formal education. So he feels hard done by, and every time he sees a picture of himself in academic dress it reminds him of what he wanted but never got. And now, with all this business about Rook's niece, he thinks that his reputation for wisdom is being undermined by the evidence of rook intelligence. I think he feels threatened by it all and he probably worries that he'll lose respect in the bird community when all this Cambridge University stuff becomes common knowledge.'

'Oh, I see,' piped Kingfisher. 'But there's not much we can do about that, is there?'

'Not really,' sang Blackbird, 'except to reassure Owl that he's a very important member of our community, and that his experience counts for a lot. He's a funny old thing in some ways, but I must admit I'm fond of him in spite of all his foibles. You know, I've heard that with humans there's sometimes a tendency for the old ones to feel undervalued, especially now that the youngsters are so savvy with their computers, and their Facebook and Twitter and TikToks and things. But I don't think there's any substitute for the quiet reflection that comes with the years, whether we're talking of humans or birds.'

Kingfisher didn't answer immediately, and Blackbird suddenly remembered that Kingfisher was very much a member of the younger generation herself, and that perhaps she felt she was being preached at by her older friend. However, Blackbird needn't have worried, for his colourful companion turned towards him, opened her beak and came out with the following thoughts:

'To tell you the truth, what I love most about life is that we're all so different. Some birds can fly thousands of miles, like the cuckoos; some are very bright, like Rook and his niece. Others can sing, like you and the nightingales, and I'm pretty good at fishing. We've all got special qualities and skills when you come to think about it.'

'Yes,' sang Blackbird, 'Woodpeckers are clever with wood and starlings can mimic lots of different sounds, like mobile ring tones and car alarms and bells and all sorts of things.'

'I know,' piped Kingfisher, 'and magpies are brilliant thieves, and Owl…well Owl can do lots of things. He's very good with words and he's a great organiser and…and…and, er…lots of things. So that's what I think, and that's it, really.'

Up in The Rookery, Rook and his niece were mulling over Owl's words and their implications.

'I must admit I didn't like the way Owl dealt with things,' croaked Rook. 'He wasn't his usual self, and do you know what I think?'

'Go on,' croaked Rachel, 'what do you think?'

'I think he's jealous of us rooks. He's jealous of our intelligence. Did you notice the way he kept closing his eyes when you were telling us about the experiments at Cambridge? As soon as he knew that it was your intelligence that was being tested he more or less switched off. That can only be envy, and that's sad because it's just a fact of life that every species has its strong points and its weaknesses. The owl may not be as clever as rooks and the other crows, but he's still quite a wise old bird and his knowledge of English grammar is second to none. *And* he can see in the dark! *And* he can swivel his neck two hundred and seventy degrees without strangling himself! And he's pretty good at holding meetings, so why can't he just accept that that's life and stop feeling so insecure? For a bird of his age, it seems ridiculous to harbour such feelings, especially when he's a pillar of society, respected by all of us and even thought of with affection by some.'

'Well, Uncle,' croaked Rachel, 'you may well be right about Owl and his reaction to what I said, but don't you think it might be the case that he's a bit of a misogynist, and his resentment might have been due as much to my gender as my intelligence? I mean, he does seem very traditional in his ways, and he may be of the opinion that a female's place is in the nest, and he may think I'm a bit uppity asking to come out on the cuckoo hunt with the rest of you.'

'Difficult to say,' croaked Rook. 'He's always perfectly alright with Kingfisher, and they even exchanged Christmas gifts, spending lots of time together training for their respective outings.'

'Well maybe,' croaked Rachel, 'but with all due respect to Kingfisher, I get the impression that she's not really Owl's intellectual equal, which may make her acceptable to him. She is, after all, very pretty, with a lovely personality from what you've told me and from what I've seen for myself. So, she doesn't represent any kind of threat to him, does she?'

'Oh, I don't know,' croaked Rook. 'Sometimes I don't know what to think…about anything. It's all so confusing these days, with labels being used all the time: misogynists, ageists, sexists. I sometimes wonder what others call *me*. A humanist, I suppose!'

'What on earth do you mean, Uncle?' croaked his puzzled niece. 'Why should you be labelled a humanist, for goodness' sake?'

'Because I'm always criticising humans, of course,' croaked Rook, in a croak that sounded more grumpy than croaky, in fact.

'But that's not a humanist,' croaked Rachel.

'Isn't it?' croaked Rook, furrowing his insubstantial brow.

'No, no. A humanist is someone who thinks that solving human problems using reason is more important than religious beliefs. Humanists emphasise that human beings are basically good, and from what I know of you, dear Uncle, I don't think that makes you a humanist!' She laughed – a gentle, affectionate sort of laugh.

'But that doesn't make sense,' croaked Rook. 'As I understand it an ageist discriminates on the basis of age, a racist on the basis of race, so putting an *–ist* on the end of a word must make it negative. So, a humanist must be someone who has negative feelings about humans, like I do!'

'No, Uncle. It's not that simple. Does a parachutist have negative feelings about his parachute? I don't think so! Is a feminist negative about females? Not really! No, English is a funny old language, and when you think about it that shouldn't really be much of a surprise. After all, it was invented by humans, who are a pretty strange lot. And worse than that, it was invented by the English, who are an even stranger lot than most! Remember, I've been living and working with them at Cambridge for the last three years and, believe me, they're quite a rum bunch!'

'Well, I suppose you're right,' croaked Rook. 'There can be no doubt that they're a weird species. Just think of all the terrible things they've done to birds down the centuries, and yet they try to imitate us with their aeroplanes and things. And not only that, if you ever visit one of their graveyards or cemeteries you'll see angels, which look just like humans but *with wings*! So although they've persecuted us for generations it seems that they idealise us at the same time! How peculiar is that!'

'They *are* peculiar, there are no two ways about it,' croaked Rachel, 'but some of the things that humans do and say might seem crazy at first, but on closer examination, there might be a perfectly reasonable explanation.'

'I'm not convinced,' croaked Rook. 'For example, why do humans (the English ones, anyway) call a castle a rook when they play chess? Doesn't make sense, does it?'

'Well some of the Cambridge humans played chess and I discovered that the word "rook" in chess comes from the

Persian word "rukh" which, believe it or not, means a fort or a castle.'

'Well I never!' croaked Rook, who was becoming increasingly impressed with his niece's erudition.

'Alright then,' he croaked, 'what about them calling a colony of penguins a rookery? Where's the logic in that?' He looked straight into Rachel's eye, and to his amazement, she came straight out with a plausible explanation:

'Uncle, I can't be sure, but think about it. Penguins, like rooks, are very social birds. Just like us, they live close together in large numbers and they communicate with each other all the time. And not only that, if you look at a penguin you'll see that its beak is very similar to our beaks and their eyes are quite like our eyes, so put all those things together and it doesn't seem quite so outlandish to use the word rookery for penguins. And anyway, I take it as a compliment to us rooks, naming colonies of penguins after us!'

'Well alright, you win,' croaked Rook. 'And not only that, you've also helped me to make what might otherwise have been quite a difficult decision. You've convinced me that you're an exceptionally gifted young bird – a credit to the species and to my family. Your parents would have been so proud of you. And the decision I've made is that tomorrow I shall stay here in The Rookery and you will join my three friends on their mission to interview the cuckoo. I'm certain you'll do a better job than I would, so I'm more than happy to let you go and see what you can find out about the mysterious migrant.'

And with that he hopped from the branch they were perched on to a lower one, making it more than clear to his niece that the decision was final and the conversation had come to an end – for the moment, at least.

Chapter Seven

As arranged, they met up after lunch the following day, exactly twenty-four hours after Rook and his niece had been cold-shouldered by Owl. When you think about it, it seems rather odd that a bird without shoulders could be capable of cold-shouldering anybody, but Owl, as everyone knew, was an anomalous bird, so his behaviour had to be judged on its own terms. Kingfisher was ready when the others arrived outside her home – first Blackbird, then Owl and finally Rachel, Rook's very clever niece. She was greeted warmly by Kingfisher and Blackbird and politely by Owl. No reference was made to Rachel's absent uncle and, after a brief exchange of views, it was agreed that they would search for the cuckoo in the same area where they'd had their previous encounter. They flew off and soon found the tree where they'd perched before talking with the cuckoo last time. They settled on the same branch and waited, and waited. It was a long wait and they hardly spoke, fearful that any noise might frighten the cuckoo off if he chose to pass that way. Ironically, their demeanour resembled nothing so much as a group of twitchers – those singular birdwatchers who travel around then hide and wait to try and spot an unusual bird, so that they can tick off its name on a list and brag to other twitchers that they've seen a red-rumped this or a middle-spotted that in such and such a wood, and aren't they just the greatest twitchers in the land! That's what our four birds looked like as they sat and waited. If they'd indulged in a bit of self-analysis, they'd most likely have concluded that they were behaving like conspirators, lying in wait for the victim of their plot, but the "victim" was proving to be characteristically elusive. Cuckoos were notoriously difficult to see, but this one was turning out to be just as hard to hear. The wood was full of all the usual sounds – the fluttering of leaves in the breeze, the rustling of small animals in the undergrowth and, unfortunately on this occasion, the obsessive cooing of a couple of collared doves, the one quite close, the other some distance away, one calling to the other, the other calling back like a brainless thing, like an echo – time after time after time! It's quite an attractive bird to look at, the collared dove, with its grey pink feathers and the distinctive black band on the back of its neck, and when it came to Britain as an immigrant in the 1950s it was possibly welcomed by some and probably ignored by most, but there must be many a man and woman in these islands who now wish it had stayed in the Middle East and Asia instead of colonising gardens and farmlands and everywhere, because if ever a bird deserved to be garrotted by its own collar it has to be the collared dove. And if that garrotting were to be carried out by a human it would probably be a very rare instance of human behaviour condoned by the bird population at large, for it's hard to believe that that constant cooing is not as irritating to other birds as it is to humans. Now you may or may not be a believer in the divine, but if Nature was created by God and he wanted to demonstrate the glory of his creation he could do worse than display a corner of an English wood as an example. However, sooner or later he would be obliged to point to a couple of cooing collared doves to admit that Satan had somehow intruded into his paradise and left these birds as evidence of his perverse presence, for if ever a sound had been invented for the purpose of torturing a brain it would have to be that unremitting, unchanging cooing of the wretched collared dove, repeated as it is at regularly timed intervals specifically designed, it would seem, to drive anyone, apart from another dove, to quivering distraction. In case, after all this, you are still wondering if this is a bird call you know, one you've encountered, it can be defined in musical terms as a crotchet, followed immediately by a minim and then a quaver – all of them pitched on the same note which, if you happen to have an instrument to hand, can be found precisely one octave above Middle C. But please don't try it at home. It could seriously damage your health!

Luckily for our little foursome, the cooing of the collared pests was suddenly interrupted by the very welcome call of the cuckoo. And surely no bird could be more deserving of its name than our friend the cuckoo. Should it happen one day that a wide-eyed child comes up to you with an innocent question, as they frequently do, and if that question should turn out to be "Mummy (or Grandad, or Auntie Mary), what does onomatopoeia mean?" – just the sort of query any small child is likely to turn up with and to worry about (I'm sure you'd agree), the answer is there – a bespoke answer, if answers can be bespoke! "What sound does a cuckoo make?" you say to the wondering child. "Cuckoo," he or she replies. "And there's your answer," you say, smiling with satisfaction at so simple a solution to so bewildering a question.

"Onomatopoeia is a word that sounds like the thing it describes, like "cuckoo" and "hiss" and "splash"," you say. And the child is happy and runs off to play without further concern in the world, until it comes up with another innocent question for the unsuspecting Auntie Mary or Uncle George. The cuckoo is such a sweet example of onomatopoeia that if our child should, upon growing up, decide to learn a foreign language the chances are that, sooner or later, he or she will discover that the distinctive call of the cuckoo has provided an onomatopoeic version for the French cuckoo: "Coucou", the Japanese: "kak-ko", the Spanish: "cuco" or even the German bird: "Kuckuck". Of course, as we all know, the Germans have, since time began, had a love affair with the consonant – any consonant, so it can surprise nobody that the Germans have managed to smuggle an extra /k/ sound onto the end of their word to make their distinctive "Kuckuck" version. Having said that, the Swedish cuckoo: "gök" is a pretty feeble attempt at onomatopoeia, and the Romanian "cuc" is half-hearted, to say the least. What in heaven's name were the Romanians thinking to call their bird "cuc" without an "oo", when everyone knows that the cuckoo says "cuckoo", not just a pathetic, monosyllabic "cuc"! But there it is, onomatopoeia is alive and well over most of Europe and beyond, and I think we can rest assured that wherever the cuckoo flies, onomatopoeia won't be far behind!

But back to our wood! The collared doves, upon hearing the call of the cuckoo, appeared either to have been caught off balance or perhaps to have been mesmerised, because they fell silent, to the probable relief of every sentient being in the wood, and its surroundings. The cuckoo came to rest in the same beech tree as before, and the doves apparently gave up and went elsewhere, for their monotonous ditty wasn't heard again that afternoon.

'What do we do now?' croaked Rachel.

'Kingfisher will fly across and talk to the cuckoo first, and then we'll follow and engage him in conversation,' said Owl with all the outward confidence of a commander about to commit his well-drilled troops to action.

'Let's hope it works,' sang a slightly more cautious Blackbird.

'Off I go,' piped Kingfisher, and sure enough, off she went to the cuckoo's tree.

'Oh hello,' said the cuckoo, 'it's you again!'

Kingfisher wasn't quite sure whether this was meant to be welcoming or not, but she put doubt aside and went straight in, asking the cuckoo how he was and whether he'd managed to get done all the things he'd had to do.

'When your time's limited, like mine, you never get everything done,' said the cuckoo, 'but you do what you can and hope you'll get finished sooner or later. It's all about prioritising,' he added, fluffing up his neck feathers, which seemed to indicate that the word "prioritising" encapsulated the essence of his reply and that nothing more needed to be said on the matter.

Kingfisher had other ideas.

'Prioritising?' she piped, hoping for clarification, for the greater the number of syllables in a word the more confused she tended to be.

'Yes, prioritising, exactly that,' repeated the cuckoo, clarification being the last thing on his mind.

'Anyway,' piped Kingfisher, 'my friends are over there and, as we said last time, we'd like to ask you a few questions about your travels and things. Will that be alright?' She tilted her head coquettishly and fixed the cuckoo with a keen eye.

'Same friends as before?' asked the cuckoo.

'More or less,' piped Kingfisher. 'There's Blackbird and Owl, but instead of Rook there's his niece, Rachel, so we're two males and two females this time.'

'Imitating humans with their political correctness, eh? Is that what it's all about?' said the cuckoo.

'I don't know anything about politics,' piped Kingfisher, 'but if I can call my friends over, I'm sure they'll be able to answer your question.'

'Go on then,' said the cuckoo, 'but you can forget about politics and political correctness for that matter. I don't care whether you're two males and two females, or two eunuchs and a couple of hermaphrodites. The only females I'm interested in are female cuckoos, and they seem to be in pretty short supply around here at the moment.'

'Can't help you there, I'm afraid,' piped Kingfisher, who was beginning to sense that she was out of her depth. If "prioritising" and "political correctness" were terms she wasn't familiar with, "eunuch" and "hermaphrodite" were well beyond her acquaintanceship. And talking of words with Greek roots, if Kingfisher had been eavesdropping on our musings about onomatopoeia she'd have been as lost as the wide-eyed child with his innocent questions. To avoid embarrassing herself in front of the cuckoo she simply got on with the matter in hand. 'I'll call my friends, then,' she piped, and call them she did.

The other three flew straight over, settling on the lower branch, like last time. Kingfisher was perched on the same branch as the cuckoo, so the seating arrangement was exactly

90

as before, in keeping with the cuckoo's wishes. No point in antagonising a bird that had seemed prickly on the previous occasion and whose secrets they genuinely wanted to discover.

'So, what can I do for you?' said the cuckoo in a matter-of-fact sort of way.

'Well, first of all, I'd like to introduce myself,' croaked Rachel. 'We haven't met before, but you *have* met my uncle.'

'Oh, don't worry about that. All birds with black feathers look the same to me,' said the cuckoo. 'Especially at night!' he added, and then he chortled, clearly convinced that he was the wittiest bird in the land.

Blackbird thought the so-called joke was in rather poor taste, but contented himself with a single, discreet tut, which went completely unnoticed by the cuckoo, who was still chortling away on his branch.

'Well,' said Owl, 'you were telling us about the satellite tracking device you have on your back and how you're co-operating with the humans in the interests of research.

'Indeed, I was,' said the cuckoo. 'So, what else would you like to know?'

'Well I'd like to know where you go when you leave England,' sang Blackbird.

'After you've fulfilled your paternal duties,' added Owl, with more than a hint of irony.

'My only duty is to father new cuckoos, to keep the species going,' said the cuckoo, making it abundantly clear that, as far as he was concerned, his responsibilities didn't extend beyond the fertilisation process. Typical absent father! But no surprise, when you think about it since nest building and the rearing of the young cuckoos are duties he *and* his

91

partner unceremoniously dump on the unsuspecting foster parents year after year. However, that's a matter for later discussion.

'Maybe that's something we could discuss later,' said Owl, an unwritten agenda taking form inside the roundness of his head. 'Er, the travels,' he added, to prompt the cuckoo into starting his story.

'Well, I'm not sure how geographically aware you birds are, but when I leave here, I head south, destination Africa. The route I take depends on a number of things, most of them related to the weather.'

'So, do you wait until the weather conditions are ideal?' croaked Rachel, anxious to get the full picture so that she'd be able to brief her uncle when she returned to The Rookery.

'In England! Where've *you* been living for the last few years?' asked the cuckoo, his tone laden with sarcasm. Little did he know that Rachel had been living in an ivory tower in Cambridge for the last three years and, as a result, had been sheltered from many of the vagaries of the English weather. 'No, no,' the cuckoo continued. 'In this place, you have to take your chances. If you hang around in England waiting for ideal weather conditions you'll never get away! And then your holiday's gone for what the English call a burton!'

'So which route did you take last year?' sang Blackbird.

'Last year, er, let me see. Yes, last year I went across the Channel and down through Germany and Switzerland to Italy. Funny place, Switzerland! They've got their own religion, the Swiss. It's called punctuality, and the god they worship is the cuckoo, so everywhere you go you see these little shrines to punctuality, which they call clocks, and they all have a cuckoo inside. Funny people, the Swiss! Anyway, after having a bit of a rest in Italy I went over the Mediterranean to Libya. That was a very popular place for humans not long ago. They were all fighting over it for some reason. Looks pretty unsavoury to my way of thinking. Just a load of sand piled up all over the place. A sort of giant building site waiting for the bricks to arrive. But that's humans for you. They'll fight over the queerest things.

'So, if Libya's such an uninspiring place, why do you go there for your annual holidays?' croaked Rachel, puzzled that any bird would want to leave England at all. No punctuality fundamentalists here, not too many cuckoo clocks either, and very little sand.

'Oh, I don't stay in Libya all that long. I don't know whether you've ever heard of Travelodge, but in Libya, there are things called oases and they're a bit like Travelodges in a way. I just stop over at a few oases to get a short rest, a drink and a bite to eat and then I'm off on my travels again. It's more or less what humans do at Travelodges, apparently.'

'So where do you go next?' piped Kingfisher, who didn't like the sound of a country that was full of sand. Couldn't be many fish in a place like that.

'After Libya, I went to Chad last year.'

'And what's Chad like?' sang Blackbird.

'Dry mountains and desert in the north and savannah in the south,' said the cuckoo.

'What's savannah?' piped Kingfisher.

'Oh, that's grassland for miles and miles and miles. And there are rivers and there's a big lake called Lake Chad. You'd love that. It's full of fish,' said the cuckoo.

'Maybe I would, but I'm happy here,' piped Kingfisher, who had no desire to leave her little river in her little piece of England.

'So, is that where you stay – in Chad?' croaked Rachel, who thought so much travel must be extremely debilitating. It made her feel tired just hearing about it.

'No, no, no. I've still got over a thousand miles to fly after Chad. First I go to the Central African Republic and finally to the D.R.C.'

'What's the D.R.C.?' asked Owl, Blackbird and Kingfisher in harmony. Rachel looked as if she already knew. Three years at the University of Cambridge does that for you, I suppose!

'It's the Democratic Republic of Congo and it's mostly tropical rainforest, so there's lots and lots to eat,' said the cuckoo. 'There are creepy crawly things everywhere, so it's a great place to fatten up after a five-thousand-mile flight. Even humans complain about the food on flights, and they don't have to flap their arms or anything, so you can imagine what it's like for birds like me who have to work all the time we're flying, and we're on limited rations. We lose lots of body weight and have to make it up as quickly as we can. And that's why we choose the Congo. Plenty of food there.'

'So, tell us more about the satellite thing you've got on your back,' said Owl. 'What happens to that while you're doing all this travelling?'

'Nothing happens to it. It just sends signals back to the ornithologists telling them where I am. Before they had these tracking devices nobody in England knew exactly where I went for the winter, but now they've been able to trace my flights for two years, so they know much more about me and my fellow cuckoos. The only thing is, when I'm in the Congo the rainforest's so dense that there isn't really enough light to recharge the solar battery, so the ornithologists don't know where I am for a while. In fact, they don't even know whether I'm alive until I start my return flight to England.'

'And when do you start your return flight?' croaked Rachel, incredulous that a bird could travel so far every year.

'I always start in February, which gives me just enough time to get back here for April. When I leave the Congo I usually make my way to Cameroon. Excellent food in Cameroon. Most of the country used to be a French colony, you know, which is why the food's of such high quality. The best caterpillars in West Africa, if you ask me. I just eat and eat and eat, and then I've got most of the fuel I need to get me back to England. Of course, I top up wherever I can, and after that, I just have to hope the tank doesn't run dry before I reach this little old wood where you folks hang out.'

'You didn't mention Cameroon on your way down to the Congo,' said Owl, who had been paying close attention to all the details the cuckoo had recounted.

'That's because I didn't go there,' laughed the cuckoo, who was once again enjoying being the centre of attention, and felt more than a cut above these parochial birds. 'On the return leg, I follow the rains, which is why I go to Cameroon. After that, it's serious flying, over northern Nigeria, all the way across Niger and then back into Libya. By the time I get here, to your charming little wood, I've done a round trip of ten thousand miles. What do you think of that?'

'I think you're brilliant,' piped Kingfisher. 'I don't know how you do it!'

'Most impressive,' sang Blackbird. 'Most impressive.'

'Er, we wanted to ask you a little bit about your family life, if you don't mind,' said Owl, 'but I get the impression that our friend, Rook's niece, has something to ask you first.'

'Yes, I do,' she croaked. 'I was wondering if any of the tracking devices are carried by female cuckoos, or is it only the males?'

'Only the males. Only the males,' said the cuckoo. 'The thing is, we're bigger and heavier and stronger than the females, so they'd struggle to carry a five-gram device on their backs, but we hardly even notice it.'

'I see. Thank you,' croaked Rachel, apparently satisfied with the cuckoo's explanation.

'So, about your family life,' said Owl, as though the four words constituted a well-crafted question, or even a question of any kind.

'What about my family life?' said the cuckoo, as if butter wouldn't melt in his beak.

'Well, for a start,' said Owl, 'we were wondering whether you had any qualms about the cuckoo practice of never building your own nests for your own offspring?'

'Qualms?' said the cuckoo. 'Why on earth should we have qualms?'

'Well,' said Owl, 'of all the bird species on the planet you seem to be the only one which steals the nests painstakingly built by other birds for their own families.'

'A misunderstanding. A common misapprehension. A frequently peddled calumny,' said the cuckoo, whose use of such vocabulary eliminated Kingfisher from the discussion at a stroke.

'How can it be a misunderstanding?' croaked Rachel, who felt that Owl needed some support against the rather formidable cuckoo.

'Because we don't steal any nests. We merely utilise them for a brief period, allowing the owners to continue to be the custodians and even entrusting our children to their care. I can't think of any other bird which is so trusting of others that it would allow total strangers to take full responsibility for the nurturing and upbringing of their own precious offspring.'

'With respect, that sounds like sophistry to me,' croaked Rachel, whose extended sojourn in Cambridge appeared to have endowed her with a generous helping of confidence.

'One bird's sophistry is another bird's rationale,' replied the cuckoo. 'It's all in the eye of the beholder. I'll tell you why we don't build nests. It's because we don't have time or energy to build them after all the miles we've travelled to get here.'

'Well the swallows and the swifts seem to find the time and energy to build nests, and they migrate just like you,' said Owl, believing that he was trumping the cuckoo's argument at one fell swoop, without actually having to swoop at all.

'Ah, but there are a number of things you need to take into account, Mr Owl,' said the cuckoo. 'First of all, consider the difference in size between us. Swifts and swallows are half our size, and they are designed for speed, so migration for them is a quicker and far less arduous undertaking than it is for us. Comparing a swift or a swallow with a cuckoo is like comparing a fighter jet with a jumbo. Our fuel consumption is far greater than theirs, so by the time we get to England our bodies are exhausted, while the smaller birds can quickly recover what they've lost, giving them ample time to build a new nest or, more commonly, repair last year's accommodation. Another thing is that swifts can actually sleep while they are in flight, so think how much migration time that must save them. No, I'm sorry Mr Owl, but your arguments are specious. You're hooting up the wrong tree.'

'Well, what about your habit of throwing other birds' eggs out of their own nests in order to substitute them with a cuckoo egg? Isn't that infanticide?' croaked Rachel, who was showing herself to be quite a feisty individual, willing to enter the fray and stand up to the summer visitor. It was clear she'd benefited from her years at Cambridge in more ways than one.

'Of course it isn't infanticide,' said the cuckoo. 'Infanticide is killing a baby, and an egg isn't a baby, is it? Do you really think all those humans are committing infanticide every morning when they crack open their breakfast eggs?'

'You know perfectly well that the eggs humans eat haven't been fertilised, so there's no comparison,' croaked Rachel. 'The eggs you remove from their nests contain embryos, so they're potential nestlings, future birds. You kill them before they even get a start in life!'

'Now look,' said the cuckoo. 'I don't want to split feathers, but it's not actually me who does any of this egg disposal. It's my better half, to coin a human phrase. I don't wish to pass the buck, but you need to get your facts right, young Miss Rook!'

'Shame on you! Shame on you!' croaked Rachel, whose hackles had been well and truly raised by the cuckoo's patronising attitude towards her and by his putting the blame on his partner. 'Not only are you guilty of murder, but you are so cowardly that you wish to place the responsibility for your crimes on the shoulders of the female of your species instead of accepting that it's a cuckoo crime, not a female crime.'

Owl was beginning to feel uncomfortable at the way the discussion was developing. Indeed, it could no longer be deemed to be a discussion, not even a robust one, for Rachel's verbal onslaught had caused it to grow into a full-blown argument. Kingfisher was amazed at the boldness being displayed by her fellow female, and Blackbird was equally taken aback. Before the cuckoo had a chance to respond to Rachel's inculpation, Owl managed to intervene, in an attempt to lower the temperature a little.

'I think we're getting a little excited here,' he said. 'Perhaps we should spend just a few minutes in quiet contemplation, with our eyes closed. It's a method used by owls all over the country. In fact, I believe it to be common to owls all over the world.'

'I don't give a hoot,' said the cuckoo. 'To be honest, I don't care two hoots about your owl meditation methods,' he said, pleased with his choice of words. He wondered if Owl had got it. 'I don't intend to sit here and be insulted by this young rook, this raucous crow, this provincial upstart. How dare she accuse me of murder and cowardice! How dare she!'

'Well I do dare,' croaked Rachel, who was preparing to sling a few insults back at the cuckoo. 'If it's name-calling you're after I think we can manage a few choice specimens to throw in your direction, Mr Cuckoo. How about "brood parasites" for starters! Everyone knows that's what you are. You're parasites on the poor unsuspecting meadow pipits and reed warblers and, in this very wood, the dunnocks.'

'What the devil's a dunnock?' said the cuckoo, whose education, despite all his travels, seemed to be inferior to that of Rook's niece, if the nomenclature of bird species was anything to go by.

'Er, the dunnock is also known as the hedge sparrow,' said Owl in as calm a voice as he could manage, hoping that calmness might spread into the atmosphere and cool a couple of tempers in the process.

'Well if she means hedge sparrow, why she doesn't say hedge sparrow?' said the cuckoo in the most sarcastic tone he could muster.

'Because any half-educated bird would know that a dunnock is another name for a hedge sparrow,' croaked Rachel. 'Its Latin name is "Prunella modularis", but I imagine it would be asking far too much of a cuckoo to be acquainted with the classical languages!'

'Bah, dead languages – of no use to a modern bird like a cuckoo!' said the cuckoo. 'As far as I'm concerned it's a sparrow.'

'Ah, but that's exactly where you're wrong,' croaked Rachel. 'And that's precisely where Latin comes in handy. The hedge sparrow, or dunnock, is not a member of the sparrow family at all, which is why I prefer to call it a dunnock. It's a member of the Prunellidae family, whereas the other sparrows, the real sparrows, are the Ploceidae family. Completely different species, Mr Cuckoo.'

'Well, just between the five of us, I don't really care. I don't give a damn about your dunnocks and your sparrows and your fancy Latin names. It's all highfalutin nonsense as far as I'm concerned.'

'Ah, but that's just where you're wrong again,' croaked Rachel, 'because in this wood it's always the poor little dunnock that falls victim to your wickedness. It's the very bird you *do* give a damn about because it's the one in whose nests you cuckoos choose to lay your eggs every year, as a result of which the poor bird loses its own eggs. And it's the little dunnock which spends all its time frantically finding food for your gluttonous progeny and pushing it down their insatiable throats.'

'What's gluttonous progeny?' piped Kingfisher in a muted tone to Blackbird, the two of them having become mere spectators to this gladiatorial contest between Rachel and the cuckoo.

'I'm not sure, but I think it means greedy children,' sang Blackbird in equally hushed tones to the grateful little kingfisher.

'Well,' said the cuckoo, 'I don't know whether you're familiar with the human expression about pots calling kettles black, young Miss Rook, or whether you know anything about a book called The Bible, where the hero says "Let him who is without sin cast the first stone", but I think both those sayings have a certain relevance here, with regard to you and me.'

'What's your point?' croaked Rachel. 'What exactly are you trying to say?'

'My point is this. You, as a rook, are hardly the right bird to be pointing your claw at me when it comes to behaviour towards others. Everyone knows that black neighbourhoods are rowdy, lawless, crime-ridden places where no respectable being can get a moment's peace. It's non-stop cawing and croaking, bickering and mayhem in the rookeries of this world, and you know it.'

'And where's the crime you talked about?' croaked Rachel, who couldn't, in all honesty, deny that rookeries were noisy places but who deeply resented the bigotry issuing from the hypocritical beak of the cuckoo.

'Huh! Who hasn't seen the bully-boy tactics of you rooks harassing a solitary red kite over England's otherwise gentle countryside? Even a single rook will attack an innocent red kite as it wheels and soars in the sky. To everyone else, it's an object of beauty and grace, but to your lot, it's a target for criminal assault. Okay, so the red kite is a much bigger bird than a rook, but it's less manoeuvrable, which makes it vulnerable to your kind of thuggery. Many's the time I've heard the plaintive cry of a kite as it tries to fend off a brazen rook or a whole gang of you, so I suggest you put your own house in order before you sit there in judgment, pretending you're a paragon of virtue, croaking out your accusations at me and my fellow cuckoos.'

'Er, if I may,' said Owl, attempting once more to be the peacemaker, 'if I may make a suggestion…'

'You can stick your suggestion up your tree trunk, as far as I'm concerned,' said the cuckoo. 'Let's hear what your young female friend has to say in her defence, shall we?'

'Indeed, you shall,' croaked Rachel, who stretched to her full size before making her riposte. 'My defence is precisely that, a defence. If a red kite comes near our rookery it represents a threat to our young, so we have to chase it off until it's well away from our airspace.'

'Huh,' said the cuckoo, 'I've never heard of a red kite eating baby rooks, and even if they did, I've seen your Blackshirts attacking them at all times of the year, not just in the nesting season. So how do you explain that?'

'Very easily,' croaked Rachel. 'It's called deterrence, or taking pre-emptive action. You've never seen a red kite eating a baby rook precisely because, unlike you, we have a reputation for taking care of our young and we make sure they're protected at all times. So there!'

'Ah well, there you have it,' said the cuckoo. 'If it's reputations we're talking about, may I refer you to the reputation you've acquired in this country, and in other countries for that matter. What was it Shakespeare called you? Birds of ill omen, if I'm not mistaken. And folklore is full of examples of the same.'

'Aha, Mr Cuckoo, so now it's time for you to get *your* facts right because in "Macbeth" and in "Othello", which I presume are the plays you're referring to, the so-called bird of ill omen is not the rook but the raven.'

'Agh! Rook, raven, crow, what's the difference!' said the cuckoo. 'You're all black and you're all troublemakers.'

'I'd like to say something,' sang Blackbird, suddenly finding his voice, so angry was he with the attitude being displayed by the cuckoo. 'You, Mr Cuckoo, are guilty of stereotyping. You don't seem to be aware that we're living in the twenty-first century. You should know that we're a bit more enlightened than we used to be. Even humans are beginning to move in the right direction! Some of them, anyway! You don't judge by the colour of the feathers. You look at the inner being. That's what counts.'

'So why is it that nearly all references to the colour black have negative connotations?' said the cuckoo, quick as ever with his challenges. 'The black market, Hitler's Blackshirts, the black economy, the Black Death, black humour, black clouds, black looks, black magic – I could go on!'

'You already do!' croaked Rachel.

'I thought Black Magic was everyone's favourite chocolate,' piped Kingfisher. 'For humans, anyway.'

'Now listen, Mr Cuckoo. We can play that sort of game too, you know,' croaked Rachel, preparing for yet another skirmish with the belligerent cuckoo. 'Here's a question for you: What do humans call someone found where they shouldn't be? Answer: A cuckoo in the nest. And here's something else for you to ponder: you were talking about folklore a few minutes ago. Well gypsies are pretty strong on folklore, and gypsies believe it's good luck to have a colony of rooks on your property, and if the rooks should suddenly abandon their rookery, disaster will follow. So, Mr Cuckoo, you are living in cloud cuckoo land if you think you can intimidate us with your spurious claims and your false reasoning.'

For once the cuckoo didn't respond, and none of the other birds made a sound. It was as if Rachel and the cuckoo had fought each other to a standstill, and just like the protagonists, the spectators were catching their breath and wondering what would happen next.

Chapter Eight

They all knew it was the cuckoo's turn to speak, but he kept them waiting for several minutes before resuming the debate, if debate it still was. Eventually, he looked each of the other birds in the eye, first Kingfisher, then Blackbird, Owl and finally, his main antagonist, Rachel. He peered deep into the glistening jet-coloured eye of the young rook and allowed his eyes to linger, as if by holding his gaze he might somehow see into the soul of his adversary – if rooks have souls, that is. He was trying to work out a way of getting the better of his smart opponent. Somehow, he needed to outwit this clever-claws, this fiery female, this quick-witted crow. Whatever it was he saw in the depths of Rachel's eye it seemed to have an effect, for instead of taking up where he had left off by delivering yet more brickbats and vitriol, he now addressed his audience in a style which could only be described as conciliatory. The tactics were turned upside down. Instead of attack, the approach was now sober, measured and emollient.

'Friends,' he started, 'allow me to put my case in a slightly different way. I understand your point of view and I acknowledge that my species, the cuckoo, is known for its unorthodox parenting style…'

'Unorthodox parenting style! That's as good a euphemism as humans calling police dogs crowd engineers,' croaked Rachel, who was clearly geared up for what she saw as round two of the bout.

'Er, just a moment,' said Owl, aiming a disapproving look at Rachel. 'I think it would be appropriate and courteous to allow the cuckoo to finish what he wishes to say. Please continue, Mr Cuckoo.'

Rachel looked surprised and chastened by Owl's intervention, and held her tongue, while the cuckoo resumed his speech.

'As I was saying, our parenting methods, as cuckoos, are unusual, unique even, but I'd like you to consider matters in their context.' He put on his most serious voice and tried to sound as authoritative as possible. 'I'm sure you all know about Darwin's theory of evolution,' he went on, 'and I guess you know that he used birds as examples.' He looked into the faces of his audience and, with the possible exception of Kingfisher, he thought they were with him so far. 'Well, if I may go into just a little detail, the birds that are now known as Darwin's finches, which the great man found in The Galapagos Islands, are all thought to be descendants of a single pair, blown across from the South American mainland less than a million years ago, and in that period of time they've evolved into thirteen separate species. Isn't that fantastic?' Again, he looked up to check that they were following his story. 'The thirteen species all have different kinds of beaks because they eat different things.' The audience still seemed to be paying attention. 'Some of them eat insects,' he continued, 'others, seeds; some eat leaves, some eat flowers, and there are others which get their food by removing ticks from the giant tortoises, and there's even a species that drinks blood by pecking into the skin of seabirds. What do you think of that?' he said with a flourish, as if he were Darwin himself, addressing a learned society.

'It's all very interesting, I'm sure, but what's it got to do with us?' sang Blackbird, who'd never really shown much interest in science. He'd always been more inclined towards the arts, particularly music, at which he excelled, of course. 'What's all this got to do with us?' he repeated, 'and what's it got to do with what we were discussing earlier?' He was beginning to feel that the cuckoo was trying to distract them from the real issues and to divert them from their own agenda. He remembered Rook's words after their last meeting, when he'd said that cuckoos were interesting birds, but not to be trusted.

'What's it got to do with us?' said the cuckoo, mimicking Blackbird. 'I'll tell you what it's got to do with you and with me. It is that just as the thirteen species of Darwin's finches all have their own distinctive feeding habits, every species of bird has its own family arrangements, and it's no good you attacking us cuckoos because we don't rear our young like you do. We've evolved to do it the way we do and that's just that. We can't be blamed for the path our evolution has followed. There are reasons behind it, and the fact that cuckoos still exist in the world must mean that it's been a successful strategy, so far at least.' He looked at the other four birds to see their reactions, and the fact that there was no immediate challenge from any of them encouraged him to elaborate on what he'd already said. 'The thing is we're all products of our separate evolutionary roads. You, Mr Owl, normally sleep during the day so that you can hunt at night, and that's been successful for you. You've got big eyes to help you see in the dark, and that means you can hunt and catch and eat the creatures that are out and about at night, while the rest of us are sleeping so that we can be fresh to do our hunting and feeding in the daytime. We're all different because we've evolved in different ways so that we can specialise. And that's the beauty of it.'

'I see what Mr Cuckoo means,' piped Kingfisher, to everyone's surprise. 'Do you remember, Blackbird, only the other day I was saying that I loved the fact that we're all so different and that we all had things we were good at and other things we couldn't do?' And it was true, wasn't it? Kingfisher had been saying that she could catch fish, and Rook was clever, and Blackbird could sing and Owl was good with words. Kingfisher didn't know the science behind it all, but the cuckoo's explanation did seem to make sense, and Kingfisher was eager to hear more. Blackbird, too, could see the logic in what the cuckoo was saying, and as for Owl, he'd enjoyed being used as an example of specialist skills, which he'd always known he had but had never really thought about before. Rachel, with her university background, knew that the cuckoo's words were right, but a part of her regretted that she couldn't continue her verbal jousting with a bird who was now talking so much sense. After all, you can't really have a fight with someone you agree with.

'So, my good friends,' said the cuckoo, 'I think we can go along with the fact that we all do things in our own ways because our evolution has pointed us in different directions. What we really need is another Darwin to explain some of the mysteries that still remain. Because there's no doubt that there are many, many things which neither we nor humans have got to the bottom of.'

'What kinds of things are you referring to?' said Owl, who was secretly hoping that the cuckoo might be about to comment on some other characteristic of owls that could make them seem even more distinctive and wonderful than they were already considered to be.

'Well, let's take instinct, for example. Why is it that we cuckoos, like a number of other species, have an instinct to migrate between here and Africa every year? Nobody told me to do it. My parents didn't even show me the route. I went on my own, not very long after being born, and I've done it every year since. Isn't that incredible?'

'It really is incredible,' piped Kingfisher, who only ever ventured away from her precious river to attend the meetings with her friends in the wood – a journey of about half a mile, and that just a few times a year. And even those little trips are not normal behaviour for kingfishers. Compare that with the ten-thousand-mile journeys which the cuckoo undertakes every year. As the cuckoo said, and as Kingfisher agreed, it certainly is incredible.

By now, the cuckoo was convinced that his strategy of conciliation was paying off. He could see that the other birds were no longer hostile towards him. On the contrary, they were calm and receptive to his message. He had succeeded in winning them over by behaving in a cool and rational manner, and even the argumentative Rachel appeared to be at ease, if not necessarily on his side. That being the case, he considered it safe to broach a sensitive area, to return in fact to the topic which had pitted the two sides against each other with such vigour only a few minutes before.

'Now, if I may, I would like you to reflect on something we were talking about earlier, namely the way we cuckoos behave towards the hedge sparrows, or dunnocks as you call them, and the pipits and the reed warblers.'

The other four birds pricked up their ears, metaphorically speaking, wondering if the cuckoo was about to resume the fight, launching into round two, having lulled his opponents into a false sense of security by behaving so reasonably and with such decorum. Rachel, in particular, braced herself for action, sensing that the others would depend on her to fight their corner, should the need arise. The cuckoo, however, continued to speak as quietly as before, looking at each bird as he delivered his carefully considered words.

'In my particular case, what I'm about to say refers to the dunnocks, but for other cuckoos, it could be the reed warblers or the meadow pipits. Now we all know that dunnocks are a common species. There are far more dunnocks than there are cuckoos, so the fact that a very small number of dunnock eggs are sacrificed in order to ensure the survival of the cuckoo species is, without my wishing to sound unsympathetic or callous, a small price to pay.' He hesitated, gauging the reaction of his listeners. 'After all,' he continued, 'most biologists believe that species diversity is a good thing, and the extinction of species, though inevitable in some cases, is something to be regretted. That being the case, it's in everyone's interest that cuckoos continue to inhabit the world and, if I may personalise the discussion, it's for the common good that I (and my partner – whoever she may turn out to be) should visit this pretty little wood once a year, to give the place a tad more diversity and, at the risk of sounding pompous – please forgive me, a touch of exoticism.'

'That *does* sound a bit pompous,' Blackbird sang quietly to Kingfisher, who nodded daintily in agreement. The cuckoo didn't appear to have heard it and went on with what he was saying.

'Now I know from what was said earlier that you are not entirely happy with what the female cuckoo does before laying her eggs. That is, you don't like her throwing out one of the existing eggs of the chosen foster parents before replacing it with an egg of her own, but this is instinctive behaviour by the cuckoo. She's not a murderer, she's simply doing what's necessary to protect her own unborn nestling. And I'm afraid what happens next may meet with even more disapproval on your part.'

'I know exactly what you're going to say,' croaked Rachel. 'You're going to tell us that when the cuckoo egg hatches the nestling pushes the other eggs out of the nest, and even throws out any other nestlings.'

'Exactly,' said the cuckoo. 'And it gives me no satisfaction to admit it, but you can surely see that this is just another example of instinct. Nobody can have told the new-born cuckoo to do such a thing but, as Darwin so succinctly put it, it's the survival of the fittest, and in this case, if the cuckoo is to get enough food to survive, the baby dunnocks must…er, how can I put it…er…go! It sounds brutal, and in a way it is, but as some other human put it: Nature, red in tooth and claw.'

'I believe the other human was Lord Tennyson,' said Owl, whose fondness for poetry was well-known in the wood.

'In his poem "In Memoriam", if I'm not mistaken,' croaked Rachel, who knew full well that the quotation came from that poem, which Tennyson had written in memory of his close friend Arthur Hallam, a fellow student at Cambridge. Whether Rachel, as a product of Cambridge herself, was identifying with Tennyson and Hallam is difficult to know, but they do say "birds of a feather flock together", so perhaps! Whatever the case, the smart young rook was certainly proving to be a rather fine advertisement for the University of Cambridge, despite her misgivings about her enforced residence in the place.

'Quite so,' said the cuckoo, without much conviction. Somehow one got the impression that Victorian English poetry was not his specialist subject or even an area of interest. Geography and science seemed to be more up his migration path, so to speak. 'Now, where was I?' he went on. 'Oh yes, I was saying that the dunnock, like the pipit and the reed warbler, is essential for our survival as cuckoos, so it follows that it's in my interest as a cuckoo for the dunnock and the other hosts to survive too. Nature seems to have ensured that dunnocks can afford to give up a very small number of eggs and nestlings without jeopardising their own survival, and by extension, the survival of the cuckoo. I'm grateful and indebted to the workings and wonders of Nature for that, and by implication, I'm equally grateful to the humble dunnock. Though it seems paradoxical, given the way that we cuckoos take action against the dunnocks' offspring, we do actually love the dunnock and the other hosts, and we want and need them to bring up healthy families of their own for the sake of their futures and for ours. And that's it, really.'

'Well,' said Owl, 'you're quite right. There is a paradox at the heart of this business, but you've made your case most eloquently and I, for one, am willing and happy to accept you as an equal member of our little woodland community and, just between the five of us, I must confess that I've always found the hedge sparrow, the dunnock, a rather unappealing species, so I'm delighted to know that they fulfil a useful purpose in Nature's grand scheme. Now, what do the rest of you think about all this?'

'I think it's all very interesting,' piped Kingfisher. 'But I want to know more about the mysteries which we need another Darwin to get to the bottom of.'

The others laughed, and the cuckoo promised to tell Kingfisher all about the mystery of pigeons, but said that it would have to wait for another day. Blackbird thanked everybody for such a stimulating discussion and Rachel nodded her head, seeming to agree with the general mood, which was a good deal more amicable than it had been. The prospects for peaceful co-existence appeared to be far more promising than some might have expected just half an hour earlier.

Chapter Nine

It was evident to everyone that the meeting had drawn to a close – there was nothing more to be said, piped, sung or croaked, so they went their separate ways, without feeling the need to make a date for a future get-together. As they flew back to their various homes Kingfisher, Owl, Blackbird and Rachel played over the words and the arguments that had been exchanged with the cuckoo, each in his or her own head, and the cuckoo himself sat on his branch going over the same debate and weighing it all up, wondering what implications, if any, there might be for himself, for his partner, when she turned up, and for the other birds in the wood.

While Rachel had been at the meeting with the others her uncle had been prancing along a stout branch near his nest, five steps to the right, five to the left; he'd been hopping down to other branches, then hopping back up again; he'd been flapping around the treetops – all of these activities physical manifestations of his mental state, which was one of considerable agitation and turmoil. He was frustrated at not being able to witness the goings-on "at first wing". He was anxious to know how Rachel was faring and he was worrying that she might not be able to give him a full account of the proceedings when she returned. However, despite all his anguish – the flapping and the hopping and the prancing, there was one part of his anatomy which failed to jump about with the other parts. Whatever the rest of his body was doing his eyes remained fixed and focused on the flight path he knew Rachel would take as she returned to the rookery. He would see her as soon as she entered the top end of the wood and he'd be there to greet her the moment she touched down after her meeting with the cuckoo and the others. Sure enough, no sooner had Rachel alighted on a branch in the rookery than Rook was by her side plying her with questions, eager to find out what had gone on, what had been said and how it had all ended. To Rook's delight and huge relief, Rachel was able and very willing to give a blow-by-blow account of everything that had taken place. There was not the tiniest detail she failed to describe, including every insult that had gone back and forth between herself and the cuckoo, the cuckoo's dramatic change of tactics halfway through the debate, Owl's insistence that the cuckoo should be given the opportunity to make his case in full and the peaceful outcome which had given everyone a sense of satisfaction and a feeling that something worthwhile had been achieved.

'I must be the proudest uncle in the rookery, probably in the whole county, perhaps even in all England,' croaked Rook, who was not only impressed with Rachel's ability to face the cuckoo and give as good as she got, but was full of admiration for her style, her spirit, her sheer mastery of the situation. 'What a girl, what a niece, what a rook!' he went on. 'And one in the eye for humans with their insulting little words and phrases: "bird-brained" indeed! We could show them a thing or two when it comes to discussion and debate! And when you think about it, comparing the size of our brains with those of humans, our intellectual capabilities are nothing short of phenomenal!'

'Now uncle, let's not go down that road,' croaked Rachel. 'I know humans aren't your favourite species, but you've got to come to terms with the fact that we share the planet with them, and since they're the ones with most of the power, the best we can do is keep out of their way as far as possible and hope they leave us to our own devices so that we can continue to do what we've always done and play our part in trying to keep nature in balance.'

There was a pause, of several seconds' duration. Rook suddenly leaned forward, his beak almost touching Rachel's.

'Hang on a minute, Rachel,' he croaked. His beak dropped open as if something had startled him. 'You've given me an idea – a really striking idea.'

'And what would that be?' croaked Rachel, a hint of scepticism in her tone. Other rooks in the rookery had told her that her uncle sometimes got a bee in his bonnet about something or other, and he could get a little bit carried away if he wasn't reined in by wiser heads. 'What's your striking idea, then?' she croaked, knowing only too well that she'd be told, whether or not she asked and whether or not she wanted to hear it.

Rook stood up to his full height and fluffed up his feathers, always a sign that he was about to proclaim something of import, in his own eyes at least.

'The thing is, because of what you and the others have achieved today in your conversation with the cuckoo, namely a fraternal attitude between all of us who live here and those who visit on a regular basis, we're in a position to act together, to unite and put forward common goals and aims.'

'I'm not sure that I follow,' croaked Rachel. 'Are you suggesting that we create a sort of co-operative, or a trade union of birds, or a socialist paradise for wildlife? It's been tried before, Uncle, admittedly not with wildlife, and not with real life, but with Orwell's farm animals, and look where that ended up!'

'No, no, no. Nothing like that! Nothing like that, at all!' croaked Rook. 'What I'm thinking is that we should make contact with humans, open discussions with them, tell them of our concerns and see if we can find some common ground so that, as you put it yourself, nature can be kept in balance and all of us can live with greater security and better prospects for the future than we have at the moment.'

'And how on earth do you suggest making contact with humans?' croaked Rachel, whose scepticism was increasing with every word that tumbled from her uncle's beak.

'Through the cuckoo, of course,' croaked Rook. 'He's got that tracking device on his back, remember, and the humans are following his every move. They know where he is at this very moment, so if we can persuade him to do something really bizarre – I mean more bizarre than the things he normally does, it would bring the humans to him to check up on him, and he could then suggest a meeting attended by all of us, giving us the opportunity to put our case to the all-powerful species, telling them about our grievances and seeing if we can get them to change some of their behaviour – their farming policies, for example, and their waste disposal methods, and their dumping of plastic here, there and everywhere, and all those gases they keep pumping into the air. What do you think? It's the chance of a lifetime having the cuckoo as a friend of ours and, presumably, a friend of

117

theirs. After all, they're working together on this tracking project, so if the humans can co-operate with a cuckoo, of all birds, why shouldn't they be able to co-operate with the rest of us?'

'Er, okay, I see where you're going, at least I think I do, but what's the really bizarre thing you're expecting the cuckoo to do to attract the attention of the humans?'

'I don't know, something really strange that takes the humans so much by surprise that they decide to track him down to find out what on earth he's up to. You're the one with the Cambridge background! If anyone can come up with something it should be you! Put your thinking cap on and see what you can magic out of that brilliant little brain of yours. Off you go, think away, as hard as you can!'

Now if there was one thing Rachel liked, it was a challenge, so she did, indeed, put on her thinking cap and, lo and behold, within the time it would take Blackbird to sing a couple of musical phrases, or Owl to blink a couple of his slow-motion blinks, she'd come up with a couple of plausible suggestions.

'What do you think of this, for starters?' she croaked. 'How about cuckoo flying in such a way that he writes the word "help" in great big letters in the sky? I don't know how sensitive the tracking device is, but it's worth a try. It would have to be in joined-up writing, so no capital letters, but I'm sure he could manage that, if we can persuade him. What do you think?'

'That's a great idea, and if it doesn't work at first, he could just keep repeating it every day until the humans realise what he's writing, and then surely they'd come and see what the problem is.'

'Or he could spell out "SOS", I suppose,' croaked Rachel. 'That might be even better.'

'Excellent! I'll fly down tomorrow and put it to him…see what he thinks,' croaked Rook.

'Er, don't you think you ought to talk it over with Owl and the others first?' croaked Rachel. 'I think they should be consulted before you talk to the cuckoo. You know how sensitive Owl is to matters of procedure, and it is something that would affect everyone if it came about, so…'

'You're absolutely right,' croaked Rook. 'Absolutely spot on. I'll go and see Owl early tomorrow morning before he settles to sleep, and if he thinks it's a good idea I'll pop in and have a chat with Blackbird and Kingfisher, and then we'll take it from there. Incidentally, I do actually think the letters would have to be massive for the tracker to register what was going on, so the cuckoo would have to fly quite a distance for it to work, but…we'll see what the others think and then we'll talk to him.'

And so, with both their heads buzzing with the thought of giant words written in invisible letters across the skies of England and the prospect of meetings with humans to discuss the future of the planet – well, the future of England, anyway, Rook and his niece settled down for a good night's sleep, brim-full of optimism and eager to get their plans underway as soon as possible.

'A radical move, if ever I heard one!' Those were the words of Owl, next morning, when he heard the details of the scheme concocted by Rook and Rachel. Although he was ready for bed, having been out hunting all night while the two rooks had been tucked up in their feathers dreaming of a new world order, the enormity of the project captured even Owl's imagination, and for at least a couple of minutes he quite forgot that it was past his bedtime.

'What a fantastic idea,' sang Blackbird when it was put to him a few minutes after Owl had given the plan his blessing. 'I think I'll try and compose a new song which could be the signature tune for a brighter future.'

Kingfisher had to be drawn away from her second-favourite activity in order to be informed of the proposed plan of action and asked for her opinion. Her favourite activity was, of course, fishing, but her second-favourite came pretty close behind. Yes, I'm sure you've guessed – flirting is what she was up to when her friends came down to the river to seek her out and, at first, she was none too pleased to see them, for her new beau was a truly splendid young bird, whose metallic sheen was a real eye-catcher, and Kingfisher was attracted to him like good old iron filings to a powerful magnet. She found this young male quite irresistible, and gave an inner sigh when she saw the delegation from the wood sweeping down towards the river. However, once the plan had been explained to her by her friend Rachel, she forgot all about love and metallic sheens, and piped with youthful exuberance:

'Rachel, you and your uncle are really brilliant! I'm so proud to have you as my friends, and I'm sure the cuckoo will go along with it, and where will it end, and maybe we'll all be famous, and we'll be celebrities and everything, and everyone will be talking about us and taking our pictures and…oh, I'm so excited!' And she really was excited by the whole thing, and the others laughed with genuine, happy laughter when they saw Kingfisher's sparkling reaction to their new idea. And now all that remained was to convince the cuckoo that their design was a good one and to hope that they'd be able to persuade him to co-operate, for without him performing a monumental piece of sky-writing and then acting as a go-between with the humans it would all come to nothing, of course.

Kingfisher's childlike enthusiasm was so overwhelming that Rachel, Rook and Blackbird found themselves succumbing to almost the same degree of excitement, and they decided there and then to fly over to the cuckoo's regular haunt so that they could sound him out and discuss the logistics of the operation, assuming, of course, that he would be amenable to the scheme and to the key role he would have to play, if it were to come to fruition. While all this frenzied planning and decision making was going on Owl, needless to say, was deeply slumbering in his favourite tree, oblivious to everything except his own owlish dreams, which may or may not have featured ambitions for some kind of brave new planet. The dreams of owls are unknown and unknowable to the rest of us, of course, but how lovely if that rather dry old bird were really to be caught up in the general fervour, if only in those dreams.

The flashy young bird who had so captivated Kingfisher, before the interruption caused by her friends, had sat on a willow branch on the opposite side of the river and watched the goings-on at first with puzzlement, then displeasure and finally dismay. This was the first time in his life that flirtation had ended in his being ignored. To be shunned when one's feathers were so exquisite, when one's blue was so excitingly electric and one's orange so warmly attractive was incomprehensible. It was an affront. It was a scandal. It was a humiliation of the first order. He flew off in disgust, a spurned lover, wondering whatever the world was coming to. Little did he know!

The committee of four: two rooks, a blackbird and a kingfisher found the cuckoo in his usual tree and, after some uncharacteristically warm exchanges of greetings and pleasantries, they broached the subject of their visit. The cuckoo listened intently and appeared to be somewhat taken aback by the ambition and scope of the business. He was, in fact, so shocked that he lost his habitual nonchalance and asked for a few minutes alone in order to consider the matter before sharing his thoughts with the others. Rook said that they would leave him to mull things over and would return the following day, if that would be acceptable to him.

'No, no! A whole night of contemplation will not be necessary,' said the cuckoo. 'We cuckoos are not birds of a meditative persuasion. In fact, religion and all things spiritual and contemplative leave us cold. We live by our wits, so we tend to make quick decisions about the everyday affairs of our lives. However, this question is very much out of the ordinary so I would value a few moments to consider the options before giving you my reaction. You may fly across to that beech tree for a short while, and I'll call you when I'm ready.'

'I'm ready,' came the cuckoo's call after no more than five minutes, and the little group re-joined him on his tree. 'I've made my decision and I'll stick to it!'

'What *is* your decision?' sang Blackbird, impatient to know the answer.

'Yes, what *is* your decision?' piped Kingfisher, like an echo.

'My decision…my decision was a difficult one…a very difficult one indeed,' said the cuckoo.

'Yes, but what is it? What decision have you made?' piped Kingfisher, unable to contain herself.

'I've decided, in the light of our recent discussions and, if I may be permitted to use a continental word, our rapprochement...'

'Oh, please tell us, what have you decided?' Kingfisher didn't know what rapprochement meant, but she certainly understood that the cuckoo enjoyed keeping them in suspense, and she didn't like it. She didn't like it one little bit.

'I've decided that it's in all our best interests to strive for a better relationship with the humans, and I've therefore concluded that it's my duty to serve as an intermediary and oil the wheels, so to speak.

'What's he talking about?' piped Kingfisher in her most hushed tones to Blackbird.

'Shh,' sang Blackbird.

'I'm prepared to attempt the skywriting task proposed by your good selves with a view to attracting the attention of the humans, and if that should succeed, I'll be willing to put your case...er, our case, and propose a meeting, or even a series of meetings to be attended by them and...er...us.'

'Hooray,' sang Blackbird.

'Yippee,' piped Kingfisher.

'Congratulations,' croaked Rook.

'Well done,' croaked Rachel. 'When can you do it?'

'Oh, there's just one little detail, just one small matter I need to draw your attention to before we can proceed further,' said the cuckoo.

The four birds looked at each other, wondering what the cuckoo was about to say next, and fearing that it might be a problem. After all, what was a small matter for a cuckoo might turn out to be a big problem for them. Just think of the egg-laying business. The "little detail" of cuckoos laying their eggs in other birds' nests was quite a big problem for the other birds! Just ask a dunnock, or a pipit or a bunting!

'The thing is,' said the cuckoo, 'I'm…er…I…er…I'm what the humans call…er…I'm dyslexic, which means that my spelling is atrocious, and that means that writing enormous letters in the sky could be horribly embarrassing for me and, I suppose, for all of us, for all birds. It could damage our reputation and give the impression that we're poorly educated, illiterate even, and…and that would…'

'Stop,' croaked Rachel. '*I'm* a pretty good speller, so I'll volunteer to fly alongside you when you're doing your writing and I'll guide you so that you do the correct spelling. What do you think?'

'Problem solved, I think,' said the cuckoo.

'Wonderful,' croaked Rachel. 'But you'll have to promise to fly slowly because speed flying is not one of my accomplishments.'

'It's a deal,' said the cuckoo. 'I think we're in business after all, my friend. And who'd have thought such a thing possible when we were having our little ding-dong yesterday!'

'It *was* quite a ding-dong,' croaked Rachel, 'but we ended the day on good terms, didn't we?'

'We certainly did,' said the cuckoo, 'so bearing all that in mind and considering this joint venture we're about to undertake, we find ourselves in a situation which some of my continental friends, the Teutonic ones, would describe as "Realpolitik", and what some of my other continental friends, the Gallic ones, would call "detente". So, as I said, it's a deal. Done! Let's shake feathers!'

And they did, and the others croaked and piped and sang in a harmonious outpouring of relief and optimism.

Chapter Ten

All that remained was to inform Owl of the outcome of the meeting with the cuckoo and to agree on a date convenient to them all for the sky-writing adventure. Of course, only the cuckoo, with Rachel as orthographic advisor, would be involved in the actual aerobatics – in the real business of writing a script (albeit a one-word script) in the heavens above the fields of England, but the others wanted to witness the spectacle and feel that they were playing a part in such an historic event.

Owl was duly informed, a day was fixed and the cuckoo and Rachel made their preparations. For the cuckoo this simply meant committing the date and time to memory, so that he'd be up and about and breakfasted, ready to take to the skies when the go-ahead was given. Owl, of course, would be the one to give the signal. He had taken it for granted that he would be the master of ceremonies, the official starter, and none of the other birds would have dreamt of things being otherwise. For Rachel, preparation consisted of putting in some serious training to try and improve her flying skills. Stamina shouldn't be a problem, for rooks often fly considerable distances to reach good feeding areas, returning en masse to their rookeries in the late afternoon or early evening, well-fed and none the worse for their commute. Speed was quite another matter, and Rachel didn't want to hold the cuckoo back too much when he was writing his message to the humans, so she set herself daily targets, flying a little further each time at her top speed so that she'd be in peak condition on the appointed day.

The day arrived and the weather was not unsuitable. England is England, so clouds were more in evidence than the sun, but at least it wasn't raining and the winds were light. All six birds assembled at the pre-arranged spot and Owl delivered a short speech.

'We are gathered here to embark on a mission which, if successful, will bring our relationship with humans into the twenty-first century.' It was typical of Owl that, despite his reference to the times we live in, his style and delivery made him sound like a minister of religion from the time of Queen Victoria. However, that was Owl, and changing him now would be like reversing the flow of the River Thames, or any other river, come to that. He continued: 'The history of our dealings with the human species, as you are all aware, is not a happy one. Today's heroic undertaking aims to put our relations, if not on an equal footing, at least on a more satisfactory basis than before. With the help of Rook's niece, Rachel, the cuckoo will attempt to make contact with humans by inscribing a word in the sky which will alert them to the fact that we have a problem. We have chosen the word "help" as our starting point, in the hope that the humans will feel obliged to respond in a favourable manner to our plea. We require a change in the way things are managed, and if the humans are not willing to co-operate, we fear the worst, for ourselves, for nature and ultimately for the entire planet. So,

Mr Cuckoo, you have our blessing. You are leaving on schedule. Enjoy your flight! And to you, Rachel, God speed!'

Owl nodded his ponderous head and the cuckoo and Rachel took to the air, while Rook, Blackbird and Kingfisher clapped their wings in a show of solidarity and to encourage the heroes in their task. Blackbird even broke into song – the new song he'd composed to symbolise a fresh start. It met with general approval, and Rook, whose knowledge of the finer details of music had benefited from his Christmas gift of tuition from Blackbird, would have praised it to the skies if they had been available. They were, of course, already occupied as the centre of everyone's attention, eight bright eyes being focused on Rachel's black form and the blue-grey body of the cuckoo as they soared upwards, becoming ever smaller shapes as the distance grew between them and their animated supporters.

Many miles were flown by the scribe and his advisor in order to write the word "help" in letters extravagant enough to stand a chance of being registered by the ornithologists following the movements of the satellite tracking device as it travelled on the cuckoo's back. When they returned home even the cuckoo was tired, for sweeping across the sky in huge arcs was not the kind of flying he was accustomed to. It didn't come naturally, and he found it quite a stressful experience. For Rachel it was thoroughly exhausting, because however much the cuckoo tried to slow his pace, he was still pushing her to her very limits. Returning safely to base was a relief for both of them, and their friends welcomed them back as if they were military pilots who'd been on a particularly challenging sortie.

The birds waited a couple of days to see if any humans would come to investigate the cuckoo's unusual aerial antics, but nothing happened. That being the case it was decided that more sky-writing attempts would have to take place, and the consensus was that the cuckoo should go out every day for a week, accompanied if necessary by Rachel, after which time a meeting would be held to discuss a strategy for the future. On his third and subsequent flights, the cuckoo decided to fly solo, for he felt reasonably confident that he could spell the word "help" correctly, now that Rachel had shown him the way a couple of times.

Six days of sky-writing were successfully completed and on the seventh, just as the cuckoo was preparing to set off on his final mission, a small group of humans were spotted by Rook as they made their way through the wood, heading in the direction of the cuckoo's tree.

'It's them, it's them, it's got to be them,' he croaked excitedly to anyone who would listen. Rachel wasn't exactly listening, but she certainly heard. 'It's worked! They've come! It's them!' he repeated.

'What's come, what's worked?' croaked Rachel, wondering what on earth could be causing her uncle to dance about on the edge of his nest in such a state of agitation.

'The humans are coming, the humans are coming. It's them. Our plan has worked. Our plan has worked!' he croaked.

No sooner had the croaks left his beak than he jumped up from the ragtag pile of twigs that passed for a nest and launched himself clumsily into the air. He flew down from the rookery and across the wood to alert the cuckoo and tell him to delay his flight, for he was convinced that these were the ornithologists on their way to investigate the cuckoo's recent aerobatics. The cuckoo readily agreed to suspend his flight, relieved not to have to repeat his writing exercise for the time being. He felt a sudden surge of something in his body. Was it adrenalin? Was it excitement? Optimism? Destiny? Could optimism or destiny surge through a cuckoo's body? He didn't know, but something certainly surged.

'My moment may have come,' he said to anyone, to everyone, to himself. 'All hopes are pinned on me. And I won't fail.'

The humans were indeed ornithologists, and they *were* the ones who had been tracking the cuckoo's movements for the last two years. So the plan had worked, they had been puzzled by the daily squiggles in the sky – squiggles being the relevant term because they hadn't been able to decipher any actual letters, let alone a word; but no matter! The crucial thing was that they'd been lured to the wood, and now that contact had been established the cuckoo had the task of communicating with them and persuading them to agree to meetings with himself and his friends.

He did a first-class job, the cuckoo, because over the next few weeks the birds, including the cuckoo, of course, spent many hours in the company of humans – a species which, as we know, comes in a variety of shapes, types and sizes. And it was not just ornithologists they met up with, but it was the ornithologists who turned out to be by far the most attractive subspecies of them all. Not physically attractive. Oh dear, no! None of the humans could be described as that, for there was not a single one who could boast a feather, a beak or a wing, or even an interesting colour – a blue, a red or a yellow. No, it was strange how unattractive the humans were – the adults at least. They seemed to be exactly the opposite of birds. With birds, the adults are exquisite examples of nature's splendour, with the possible exception of the cormorant, especially when drying himself out after a day's fishing. A sorry, bedraggled sight is the dripping cormorant! However, adult birds in general are a gift to the eye. But, perversely, the recently hatched baby bird is the very essence of ugliness. All beak and no feathers just about sums it up! With humans, on the other hand, it's the babies who are the most pleasing to look at. They have perfect, delicate skin and their bodies are softly rounded and amusingly dimpled. But the adults! Oh dear! No, no, no! From the viewpoint of a bird, the adult human is a rather unfortunate specimen, to say the least! Long thick legs, heads stuck on top of spiky necks and somewhere between them a couple of arms dangling from the top of the body and at the lower end a pair of buttocks, an odd protuberance which, one of the birds had read somewhere, is considered attractive to male humans when they are assessing females, and may even be appreciated on males by some females. And that's looking at the human just from the back! From the front, as far as the birds could see, the structure was even more bizarre, but luckily, the clothes worn by the humans hid the more outlandish parts from view. Of course, birds don't go in for peculiar appendages on their bodies, so the various bulges and pendulous parts to be found on the front of humans would have caused puzzlement, and quite possibly a few sniggers from the birds if everything had been visible, but the garments worked well enough and appeared to Owl and his friends to be a sort of feather substitute, though of a most inferior type. The birds would surely have failed to see a need for the quirky bits hidden by the clothes for they, themselves, are sleek and lovely creatures unencumbered by lumps and assorted hanging parts. So, the six worthy friends were unanimous in their opinion that humans were physically unappealing, but with regard to attitudes, respect for other species and general awareness of the problems facing nature and the planet, of all the humans they met it was the ornithologists who came out on top. The ornithologists themselves, when given the opportunity to express their views after listening to some of the grievances listed by the birds, put it this way:

'You birds are preaching to the converted. We agree with every point you're making. It's the others we've got to convince.' (By which, of course, they meant "the other humans".)

And so, there were consultations with councillors, seminars with students and meetings with members of parliament. The interesting thing for the birds was to see that there was a pecking order between the various human subspecies and even within each group, just like chickens in the farmyard (or rooks in the rookery, for that matter)! Also noteworthy was the reaction of the humans to the birds' communication skills. The ornithologists had been quick to compliment the cuckoo on his command of speech in general and his proficiency in English in particular. Most of the other humans took it for granted that the birds would speak, and that the language they spoke would be English. They would have considered any suggestion that they, as humans, should learn to speak the native language of any of the birds a laughable thing.

'The very idea that we should spend our time studying the speech of a bird! How preposterous is that! No, no. Let them speak English, which appears to be their lingua franca anyway. We'll make allowances for any imperfections, however amusing, but English it must be.' Without a doubt, that would have been the prevailing attitude.

The birds had decided that at each meeting with the humans one of them would present their case and the others would be there as back-up if necessary. Owl had decided that he would speak at the meeting with the parliamentarians. The others had drawn straws from a little pile they'd found in the corner of a field adjoining their wood. The one who'd drawn the shortest straw would speak at the first official meeting with the humans, the next shortest at the next meeting, and so on. To her horror, it was Kingfisher who'd drawn the shortest straw and she'd immediately started jumping about and flapping her delicate wings in a state of emotion bordering on panic. The others had all gathered round and gradually managed to calm her down, saying that she'd be fine and that they had every confidence in her. Rachel had whispered in her ear that she'd help her to prepare her presentation in advance of the big day, so there'd be no need to worry. However, when the day arrived, Kingfisher had such a terrible attack of nerves that Rachel had to step in and take her place. Rachel was the obvious candidate since she'd been coaching Kingfisher and knew exactly what her little friend was going to say. In truth, it was fortunate that Rachel was the first spokesbird, because first impressions do count for a lot and, as we know, Rachel was a formidable debater and would be capable of holding her own if the humans should attempt to browbeat her or try anything on.

This first official meeting was with a group of councillors who represented the local area, which included the wood and all the nesting sites of the five birds. The sixth bird, the cuckoo, didn't, of course, have a nest or a site of his own. He was technically "of no fixed abode", but his normal operating area fell within the boundaries covered by the councillors, so he qualified as a seasonal resident at least. When it was time for Rachel to make her opening remarks, she made herself as tall as she could and started her delivery:

'Ladies and gentlemen,' she began, 'if I may I'd like to take you back about five hundred years, to the time when Europeans started to colonise the New World.' The councillors looked at each other, wondering where this confident-sounding bird could possibly be taking them. Rachel continued:

'At that time there were approximately fifty million bison roaming the plains of North America, as they had since the Ice Age. By the beginning of the twentieth century, just four hundred years later, there were only two thousand bison still alive. From fifty million down to two thousand! The Europeans had slaughtered them and driven them to the brink of extinction. Now you may well be wondering why I've chosen to draw your attention to the North American bison, a creature which may seem irrelevant to our wood, our country or our times, but it is, of course, a symbol of the devastation which irresponsible human behaviour can cause to the natural order. Allow me to give you another example, this time a creature nearer to my own heart and the hearts of my fellow birds. I speak of the dodo, the giant flightless pigeon, and more than three feet tall. Can you imagine a bird of such a size? And yet the dodo was pushed over the edge, again as a result of human hunting as well as the introduction of pigs and rats to its island home of Mauritius. The dodo had lived in peace and harmony with its surroundings for millennia until the European sailors and colonisers arrived. By the mid-1600s, only a short time after their appearance on the island, the unfortunate dodo had been wiped out. Today, as you will all be aware, its very name is synonymous with the concept of extinction. Of course, we all die sooner or later. Dying is dying. But dying *out* is something rather different. The plain truth is that nothing can be "deader" than a dodo! In fact, the only place you'll find a dodo these days is in "Alice's Adventures in Wonderland", where he puts in an eccentric appearance with three other birds and several other curious creatures. I suppose the only consolation is that if reading continues to be an activity pursued by humans, then the dodo will survive in fictitious form at least, but I think you'd agree it's not quite the same…not for the dodo, anyway!'

The spokesman for the councillors stood up to comment on Rachel's opening points. He was a heavily built man with an unhealthy-looking paunch, which bulged from inside a white shirt and seemed to be inflicting an extreme stress test on the unfortunate buttons. The councillor spoke, and each time he took a breath the buttons strained to contain the prodigious belly and keep it where it belonged.

'What you say cannot be denied,' he started. 'Human hunters killed the bison and wiped out the dodo, but all that was in the past. It was a long time ago. We are now much more aware of the dangers of unregulated hunting, and overfishing, come to that. Nowadays we control these things; we have monitoring, we set quotas. We're a changed species. We recognise our responsibilities. We know that nothing should be done to excess.'

Kingfisher leaned across to Blackbird and piped quietly into his ear that she thought the councillor's shirt buttons, if they could talk, would probably say that the councillor had a habit of eating and drinking to excess, but Blackbird told her not to judge by appearances and to focus instead on what the councillor was saying. However, the councillor sat down, leaving the floor to Rachel, who continued with her theme.

'Well, with respect,' she went on, 'we birds would maintain that humans are still doing things to excess and still causing huge damage to our environment. For example, what about all the "-ides" you've been using on our fields for the last seventy years?'

'What do you mean "-ides"?' said the voice of the councillor.

'I mean insecticides, pesticides, herbicides and several more besides!' croaked Rachel.

'Oh, very good! Your niece is clever with words,' sang Blackbird quietly to Rook. 'All the –ides; herbicides and several more besides…I like it.' Rook nodded proudly.

'You're killing off the bees and the beetles and all the other pollinators,' Rachel continued, 'and if you carry on like this, we're all going to go the way of the dodo. We're all interdependent, all the creatures on the earth, and destroying one species has a knock-on effect on the others. You interfere with the balance of nature at your peril – at all our perils.'

The discussion went on in this vein for quite some time, with the councillors conceding that mistakes had been made and that some farming practices were still doing damage to the environment. Rachel succeeded in persuading the councillors to call a meeting of the local farmers to see if they might be willing to make some changes to the way they managed the land so that wildlife would be encouraged rather than threatened. Rachel said she would get together with her colleagues and present the councillors with a possible plan of action, which could then be shown to the farmers in the hope that constructive suggestions might change opinions and actually make a difference on the ground – literally, on the ground.

The birds left the meeting with the councillors, encouraged by the reception their ideas had been given and they all congratulated Rachel on a fine performance. The next meeting would be with students at the university in the nearby town and it would take the form of a presentation by one of the birds, to be followed by a seminar. This time it would be Blackbird who would represent the birds, with the others there to give their support, of course. Ideas would be discussed beforehand by all six birds and once a consensus had been reached on the points to be made and how they should be delivered Blackbird would rehearse his speech until they were all satisfied that their case would be presented in the most effective manner possible. Blackbird admitted to feeling nervous at the prospect of representing his group, but vowed to work hard and do his very best to follow the excellent example given by Rachel.

The birds flew together to the university on the agreed day and were politely greeted and welcomed by the vice-chancellor. They were shown to the lecture theatre, where a hundred or so interested students were already in place. The vice-chancellor made a short introductory speech, describing the event about to take place as ground-breaking, revolutionary even. "The first dialogue of its kind between the young people of one species and members of another species, in an attempt to find better solutions for the future of all species" was how he put it. Blackbird shuddered with nervous tension, but took his place, perching on top of the lectern and gulping down deep breaths of air in readiness for his lecture to the students. A camera lens was focused on him and the image of his entire body was projected onto a huge white screen behind where he was perched, so that everyone could see him clearly and in bold form. He looked handsome. His feathers were a perfect black against the spotless white of the screen. His beak was a deep yellow, almost gold, and his eyes glistened in the artificial lighting of the lecture room.

'Good morning to you all,' he started. 'It's a privilege to be perched here today in this place of learning and to have the opportunity to present our ideas and thoughts on the relationship between birds and humans as we see them, and then to be able to discuss some of the issues with a small group of you in a seminar to follow on from my lecture. Of course, what we are considering are not only matters of concern to birds and humans but, as your vice-chancellor rightly said, to all species. I would go even further and say that the implications affect all of nature and ultimately, planet earth as a whole.'

Kingfisher nudged Rook and piped softly:

'He's made a good start. Doesn't he look wonderful on screen? He's very photo…er…photo…er…'

'Photogenic,' croaked Rook in an equally muted voice. 'But let's listen. Let's listen to what he's saying to make sure he gets it right.'

And to his credit, Blackbird did get it right. He delivered his lecture in the clearest of tones, linking all the points he'd agreed with the others beforehand and rising splendidly to the occasion. When it was finished, the students broke into enthusiastic applause, and poor Blackbird was so startled that instinct caused him to fly several inches into the air above the lectern before composing himself and landing safely back to where he was supposed to be. The students were charmed by this delightful little sign of vulnerability which, in a way, underlined one of Blackbird's main points, that ever since humans had put in their appearance on the planet birds, like most other species, had needed to be wary and vigilant in their dealings with the newcomers because homo sapiens had shown itself to be a predatory, unpredictable and destructive creature.

Immediately after Blackbird's lecture and before the start of the seminar the birds were invited to the university refectory for light refreshments. A row of perches had been set up, one for each bird, facing a table where the vice-chancellor and some of the university's professors and senior administrators were seated. Each of the humans had a plate of food, a tumbler of water and a glass of wine, while the birds had small jars of their kinds of food attached to the perches with wire hooks. The lid of each jar had been filled with water, so that dry throats could be soothed or thirsty stomachs quenched. For Kingfisher the caterers had provided a rather fine chunk of fresh rainbow trout – raw of course; for Rook and Rachel there was an attractive assortment of grubs – wriggling and very much alive; Blackbird's jar contained a couple of extremely juicy looking earthworms, and the cuckoo's treat consisted of four chubby caterpillars – two smooth and green, and two furry and striped. Owl, for his part, had been presented with a decapitated but still warm mouse for his delectation. It was clear that the caterers, or those who instruct them, had done their homework, and done it very well, for nothing had been left to chance and the victuals provided were second to none. Owl was particularly impressed with the temperature of his mouse, which was just how he liked it, though he was more than a little puzzled by its colour, for it was pure white, and not at all like the mice he had habitually eaten in the wood. When he later commented on this to one of the university staff he was told that it was a laboratory mouse which, he had to confess, was not a species he was familiar with. Whatever it was, it was delicious, and he resolved there and then that in his future woodland hunts he would keep an eye open for laboratory mice, for they were quite an improvement on his normal fare. The laboratory species was, without doubt, a more refined taste and one which Owl found pleasing to his palate. Even Kingfisher, who was known to be quite a fussy eater, was very content with her trout, while the grub and worm eaters appeared to be equally satisfied with their respective menus. It was a fine lunch!

The seminar went very well indeed. All the birds made contributions to the discussion, and the dozen or more students who attended were positive and full of enthusiasm. They were open to new ideas and full of encouragement to the birds, praising their initiative and pledging support in the future. At the end of the seminar, there was general agreement that this must not be a one-off affair. There would be follow-up meetings and constant updates, so that ideas could be exchanged on a regular basis. All in all, it seemed to have been a highly successful day, but on their flight home from the university, Kingfisher surprised Rachel by admitting to being rather less impressed with the students than were her friends.

'How could you not be pleased with the way they applauded and praised Blackbird for his lecture?' croaked Rachel.

'Oh, it's not that,' piped Kingfisher.

'Then what is it?' croaked Rachel. 'The seminar was brilliant. We had a scintillating discussion with those students and they were on our side. They hold the same beliefs as we do. They might have slightly different priorities and some of their ideas were perhaps a bit eccentric, but all things considered, they seemed a great bunch of youngsters whose hearts are in the right place and who want the world to be a better place for us all. How can you not have been happy with all that?'

'No, I agree, everything you say is true,' piped Kingfisher, 'but I'm not sure we can trust them. We have to be very careful with humans. We all know that, from bitter experience. Your uncle has said it many times.'

'Yes,' croaked Rachel, 'but these are a new generation of humans and they can see what their ancestors did. These are bright young things, full of optimism and eager to right the wrongs of the past.'

'Well I'm not convinced,' piped Kingfisher, who was not normally considered to be a sceptical kind of bird. That was more likely to be the attitude of Rook or Owl, but there was clearly something that had provoked this reaction in her, so Rachel decided to press her a little.

'Tell me,' she croaked, 'what was it about the students that made you suspicious? It's not like you to be negative about things.'

'Well, the lecture went very well,' piped Kingfisher, 'but the students in the seminar were very strange.'

'In what way strange?' croaked Rachel, trying, as gently as possible, to coax whatever it was from her friend.

'Well,' piped Kingfisher, 'I trusted them at the beginning, but everything changed when the student who was sitting at the end of the table suddenly said she was green. And then all the others said that they were green, too. I mean, if they think they're green they must think that I'm black and white like a coot, and that you're yellow and brown like a yellowhammer! I mean, how can you trust a species that comes out with something as silly as that. We could all see that they weren't green, so why would they say such a thing?'

Rachel waited until Kingfisher had got the whole thing off her breast before replying and explaining to her that when humans describe themselves as green, they don't mean that they're green.

'They mean that they love the planet and want to save it,' she croaked, trying hard not to smile at Kingfisher's naiveté.

'So why don't they say what they mean instead of talking such nonsense and telling such lies?' piped Kingfisher, who would need quite a bit of convincing that the students weren't telling lies but were just using English the way humans do. All the way home Rachel tried to set matters straight in Kingfisher's mind and finally succeeded in persuading her that it was all just a misunderstanding of language and, at Kingfisher's request, she promised not to say a word about it to the others, because they both knew that their friends would laugh at Kingfisher if they got to hear about it, and Kingfisher didn't want to be embarrassed and humiliated, and Rachel wouldn't have wanted it either. She was genuinely fond of her little friend and found her innocence (in matters of the mind, if not the body) quite an appealing trait.

The final meeting in the series was the one they were all dreading and looking forward to at the same time. It was the meeting with the members of parliament and it was the one where Owl would be making the presentation on behalf of the birds. Owl had made that decision, and none of the other birds had challenged him. However, they were somewhat put out when he declined their offers of help in the preparation of his speech. He was unwilling even to discuss possible points for inclusion, and such words as stubborn and arrogant began to be associated with his name in informal conversations between the other birds. They worried that he might not do justice to their cause in this most important of forums, and all because he was convinced that he knew best.

'Perhaps he *does* know best,' piped Kingfisher, back to her trusting ways.

'And perhaps he doesn't,' croaked Rook and Rachel in unison, fearing the worst, but hoping for the best.

Try as they might the other birds failed completely to twist Owl's wing and get him to at least tell them what he planned to say to the MPs. Their hope had been that if they knew what he was going to say they could diplomatically suggest that this or that other item might be popped in for added effect or as a little bonus. But no! Owl wouldn't budge, dismissing every appeal with a shrug of his non-existent shoulders and a swivel of his spherical head.

'Everything's under control,' he would say, when pressed. 'I know what I'm going to say and I believe it will be effective. And that's that!'

And that *was* that, for when Owl had decided something, no amount of cajoling or pleading would get him to change his mind or even consider making a small concession here or a slight adjustment there.

So that was how things were on the day the birds set off from their wood and flew all the way to London and the famous Palace of Westminster. They arrived early, for a tailwind had made for a speedy flight. They circled around Parliament Square a couple of times, before making their descent. They had about twenty minutes to wait before they'd be admitted to Parliament, so they split into pairs and settled in three separate landing sites. Owl and Rook chose to perch on the head of Richard the Lionheart, whose statue is just outside the House of Lords. For Blackbird and the cuckoo Oliver Cromwell's statue, conveniently located outside the House of Commons, provided an appropriate holding station, leaving Winston Churchill in Parliament Square itself for Rachel and Kingfisher. Of course, Churchill wasn't the only option in the square, since there are ten statues in total, but what bird would want to sit on top of George Canning or the 14th Earl of Derby when Churchill's ample head was available, and so inviting. As for Rook and Owl, they were well pleased with their perch atop Richard the Lionheart, who was himself perched atop his horse, and Rook was delighted to be able to share his knowledge of history with his woodland friend.

'Did you know that Parliament was bombed by the enemy in 1940?' he croaked.

'I believe I did,' said Owl in an off-hand sort of way. 'It would have been a pretty obvious target, I suppose.'

'Indeed, it was,' croaked Rook, 'and this statue on which we're resting was hit by shrapnel from that very bomb.'

'Is that so?' said Owl, in a rather less nonchalant manner than before.

'Yes,' croaked Rook, 'and if you look very carefully at Richard's sword, you'll see that it's not quite straight. There's a tiny bend in it, and that is as a result of damage from that bomb.'

'Well I never!' said Owl, clearly impressed by Rook's knowledge of the historical detail, and slightly shaken to find himself sitting on a statue that had been bombed by Adolf Hitler.

'But that's not all,' croaked Rook, eager to give Owl the whole story. 'You see, shortly after this attack on Parliament which, as I said, apart from all the other damage, caused Richard's sword to bend but not break, the BBC, in an allied wartime broadcast, used the sword which is here, in front of our beaks, as a symbol of the strength of democracy, which would bend but not break under attack.'

'Well all I can say is that I hope Hitler heard the broadcast!' said Owl, who was, in his own way, quite a patriotic old thing.

The two birds spent the next few minutes looking across from their rather splendid vantage point at all the passing humans – clerical staff hurrying along with papers under their arms, foreign tourists of every possible description and dress dawdling by and taking pictures of each other in front of iron railings, or bits of building, or even the back end of Richard's horse. No doubt some of the passers-by would have been politicians of this, that or the other ideological persuasion, but neither Owl nor Rook was able to identify anyone of note. Suddenly, Owl did one of his inimitable head swivels, faced Rook and proclaimed, as if he were breaking a monumental item of news to stun the world, that this was the first time in his life that he had ever ridden a horse. Rook was startled that Owl's mind should have been focusing on such a trivial matter when, here they were, not just outside the mother of parliaments but about to address representatives of the people of this United Kingdom of Great Britain and Northern Ireland on matters of concern to every living thing on the planet. And not only that! Owl wasn't actually riding a horse anyway! He was perched on top of the bronze head of a one hundred and fifty-year-old statue of a long-dead king of England, and that metal king was sitting on top of a metal horse of a similar age. If, for Owl, that constituted riding a horse then Rook wondered what on earth might be in store for him and for the rest of the audience when Owl made his parliamentary debut within a matter of minutes. Rook's feathers gave an involuntary shiver at the prospect.

Just across the way from Richard the First and his feathery guests Kingfisher and Rachel were surveying London's traffic and general hustle and bustle from their perch on the capacious head of Herr Hitler's most determined foe. Without warning, Kingfisher turned away from all the activity, cocked her little head to one side and peered down at the portly figure she was sitting on, then raised her voice above the noise of the passing cars and taxis.

'This Winston Churchill we're perched on – he is the one who beat the nasties in the war, isn't he?'

'The Nazis. Yes, he's the one, although to be fair he didn't do it alone. He had help from Roosevelt and the fearsome Stalin.'

'I didn't know Roosevelt had a starling. Why was it so fierce? Was it trained to peck out the eyes of the nasties?'

At first, Rachel thought Kingfisher was making a joke, but of course, she wasn't. "What do I do – laugh or cry?" she wondered. Instead, she answered her little friend as if the questions had been the most natural in the world.

'No, Stalin was the name of the Soviet leader, so the Russians and eventually the Americans fought with us to defeat the Nazis,' she croaked. 'And I'll tell you something else,' she went on, 'in cartoons they often drew Churchill's face as an English bulldog, which was good because it showed him as a strong and tenacious fighter.'

'Which he was, wasn't he?' piped Kingfisher, not sure of the word "tenacious", but warming to the topic anyway, for in her own way she was proud of her heritage and very content to be an English kingfisher.

'He certainly was,' croaked Rachel, 'but I don't think he was just a bulldog, because I've seen pictures of him wearing a Siren suit, which he used to call his romper suit and, to be honest, his tubby little body looks just like an owl. So that's quite a picture, isn't it? The head of a bulldog on top of the body of an owl!' Rachel laughed at the image she was conjuring up, and Kingfisher laughed too. 'And that's not all,' croaked Rachel, 'because apparently the company that made the Siren suits had to keep making repairs to them during the war, not because of damage from enemy action but because of burns from hot cigar ash.'

'Well, who cares as long as he won the war!' piped Kingfisher.

Just then Rachel noticed that Blackbird and the cuckoo had left Oliver Cromwell and were heading over towards Richard the Lionheart.

'I think we need to go,' she croaked, and up they went, flying across to join their companions, all four of whom were now prancing along the mane of King Richard's stoical horse. After a hasty preen and a check that every feather was in place the six of them flew over the heads of the policemen who were standing around in small groups, and gracefully swerved round to the entrance of the Commons, where they were greeted by the MP for their local constituency, who had been awaiting their arrival with a mixture of mild amusement and nervous puzzlement.

'I'm afraid you'll have to undergo the usual security procedures,' he told them, apologetically. 'Well, when I say "usual" I actually mean "unusual", because instead of our normal security staff you'll be checked by a special vet we've asked to come in for the purpose. Of course, we had to vet the vet first,' he joked. The birds nodded in acknowledgement of his wit, for that seemed the polite thing to do, but the MP himself burst into such an explosion of laughter at his own linguistic dexterity that Kingfisher and Blackbird were startled into a fluttering of wings, and in the case of Blackbird a couple of involuntary squawks of warning as well.

'Oh, sorry,' said the MP. 'Didn't mean to scare you! We tend to be quite a noisy lot, us MPs, and we sometimes forget what normal behaviour is like…until we get home, that is, and then our spouses remind us in no uncertain terms.' Again, he boomed with laughter, as if he were the funniest man in England which, as far as Owl and the others were concerned, he probably wasn't. However, he was their MP, even though none of them had voted for him, avian suffrage being way over the horizon for the foreseeable future, even in Britain with its vigorous animal rights organisations.

The vet was summoned on a pager and appeared within a couple of minutes. She seemed to be both amused and bemused by the duty she'd been asked to carry out, but she got on and inspected each bird, gently pulling up their wings to check for bombs and air to air missiles, or cunningly concealed scimitars and machetes, while the MP took photographs of the whole business, presumably to show those colleagues who may have doubted the veracity of his story or the soundness of his mind, and probably, humans being humans, to provide entertainment for his mates and family at the same time.

'At least I won't need to ask you to take your shoes off,' said the vet, who seemed satisfied that the visitors posed no identifiable threat to the safety of parliament or parliamentarians. 'That's it, done!' she added, smiling at the birds and, as Kingfisher noted, giving a knowing wink to the MP, who had pocketed his camera and was now ready to escort his constituents to one of the many side rooms, where they would meet an all-party group of MPs to discuss the matters which concerned them.

'Er, I hope you won't be offended,' said the MP, 'but I'm afraid flying is not permitted within the Palace of Westminster. It's officially designated as a No-Fly Zone, and I surmise that walking along our rather extensive corridors is not an appropriate option for you, so I've arranged for Hospitality to provide a trolley – normally used for conveying cakes or canapés for visiting dignitaries or other guests,' he added with a chuckle, 'so that you can be wheeled to the room we've chosen for our meeting. Will that be acceptable to you?'

Owl said that it would, and the MP took out his pager to request that the trolley be brought down. They all waited for a few minutes, with the MP attempting to amuse the birds with numerous anecdotes about life in parliament, while all the time he was nodding and smiling at fellow members and other assorted humans who were passing them in the corridor and who were, without exception, staring at the birds in disbelief.

'I'll tell you later,' or 'All will be explained,' were the phrases that burbled from the grinning lips of their MP to some of the more inquisitive and bewildered of his colleagues who went past, as the birds waited for the arrival of the trolley. When it finally came the MP invited them to sit in a row along the metal bar at the front end, and the hospitality lady pushed them along from the back. The MP walked alongside, like a sort of outrider protecting a diminutive family of exotic royals. It was quite a spectacle, and everyone they met as they progressed along the labyrinth of corridors turned to look or just stopped and gawped in amazement.

'Seems Catering is taking its mission to provide fresh food very seriously these days,' one wag was overheard quipping to a colleague.

'I've heard of consulting minority groups, but this is PC gone mad,' said another.

The birds heard all this and several more comments in a similar vein but chose to ignore them, deciding that a show of dignity was more likely to win them friends than an angry reaction to such puerile provocation.

They finally reached the room allocated to them and found a dozen or so MPs already there. At the side of the room, sitting apart from everyone else, was a familiar figure. It was none other than the editor-in-chief and proprietor of their very own "Woodland Bugle" – the sly old, wily old newshound, Mr Fox, with a traditional notepad on his lap, and a pencil strapped to the end of his paw, poised and ready to take down notes of the proceedings in order to report the momentous meeting between the birds and the parliamentarians to all the woodland creatures back home.

One of the MPs stood up to welcome the visiting birds, who were invited to make themselves comfortable on six sturdy-looking perches which had been placed at the front of the room, facing the assembled parliamentarians – nine or ten men and two or three women. Their own constituency MP joined his colleagues and the meeting got underway. It took the form of a presentation by Owl which, it was agreed beforehand, could be interrupted at any stage by anyone in the room for purposes of clarification or for other relevant points to be added, or for challenges to be made. Rook and Rachel in particular were grateful for such a flexible format since they feared that Owl might not be on top of the facts or that he might not make their case with sufficient force and vigour. They were reassured to know that they could have their say if Owl should underperform.

Chapter Eleven

Owl started by clearing his throat, a part of his anatomy which didn't even appear to exist, but somehow he managed to clear it, wherever it was. He looked at his audience, blinked slowly a couple of times, then began his speech, calmly and deliberately, pausing briefly after each sentence as if to allow the information to sink into the human heads arranged in front of him. He said that he'd been told that up to the Second World War and for a few years afterwards British farmers had planted fields of clover in addition to all the usual crops. The clover was grown mainly as fodder for the workhorses which were employed on the land before the widespread use of tractors. When the tractors took over, the clover was no longer grown extensively, and within a relatively short period of time, a wonderful and prolific source of nectar for bees had become increasingly difficult to find.

'That,' said Owl, 'is just one example of how so-called progress can have unintended and unforeseen consequences.' He talked of changes in land management he'd seen during his own lifetime and said that the spreading and spraying of chemicals and loss of habitat had led to serious declines in the population of many insects, not just bees and bumblebees.

'And when insects disappear, the creatures that feed on insects also disappear,' he said, turning his head slowly so that he could look into the eyes of every human in the room, one after the other. 'Birds and bats are among the victims of that decline in the insect population' he said, 'but the real issue is that nature's balance is being altered and nobody knows what the long-term effects will be.'

At this point, Rook turned to look at Rachel, and like mirror images, they nodded to each other, a clear indication that Owl's introductory remarks met with their approval. Mr Fox was busy with his notepad and pencil.

'Now as we all know,' said Owl, 'the main driving force for all these changes taking place in agriculture is the massive increase in the human population. At the time of Shakespeare, the population of England was about four million. If you add fifty-two to that number, you get the current population.' He looked at his audience and noticed that two of them were sharing a little fun, and he guessed what they were up to. 'No, not four million and fifty-two people,' he said, with a wink at the two jokers. 'The population of England today is fifty-six million.' He repeated it slowly, solemnly. 'Fifty-six million. But let's consider the planet as a whole. You may or may not know these statistics, but please bear with me, for I think they need to be quoted if only to remind us of the gravity of the situation confronting us.' He looked up at the ceiling as if the population figures were written above his head, but in reality, he thought the gesture added gravitas to his bearing, while at the same time making it more difficult for one or more of the humans to interrupt him, since eye contact was avoided.

'The human population of planet earth in 1830 was one billion. A hundred years later, in 1930, it had doubled to two billion. Forty years later, in 1970, it had doubled again to four billion. Another fifty years brings us to the present day, and it's doubled again, to almost eight billion, with the likelihood that it will go up to ten billion human beings by the end of this century.' Owl was well into third or even fourth gear, and there could be no doubting his conviction or his determination to convey the information stored in his head to his distinguished audience. 'Now, as you will be aware,' he went on, 'the original cause of the increase in the human population was the cultivation of land and the domestication of animals, and those things started about ten thousand years ago. So, in terms of the history of our planet, *our* planet, our shared planet, this whole business of land management is a very recent phenomenon, but its effects have been dramatic, and in some cases catastrophic. Forests and woods have been and still are being cut down at an alarming rate in many parts of the world. I'm told that there are now more tigers kept as so-called pets by rich people in Texas than there are wild tigers in the whole world. In India, the habitat of the tiger is being eroded by the needs of almost 1.4 billion Indians, hungry for land to feed hungry humans.'

The MPs were listening intently to Owl's words, and appeared to be impressed with his command of the facts and with his presentation of them. Mr Fox was scribbling away furiously on his notepad. Blackbird and Kingfisher were experiencing feelings of deep pride in Owl's performance, while Rook and Rachel were feeling relief. As for the cuckoo, it was impossible to know or even guess at his reactions, for he was half-heartedly preening himself one moment and gazing around the room the next. Odd birds, cuckoos!

'Now, ladies and gentlemen,' Owl continued, 'I would not wish you to think that we have come here to Parliament in order to lobby just on our own behalf – that is, for the selfish and exclusive needs of birds. No, no! Our mission is much broader than that. Yes, we are concerned with the way farming is changing the landscape of England, of Britain and of the world, but we are equally disturbed that the air we all breathe and depend on is being polluted. We are just as worried about the over-fishing of the seas. North Atlantic cod disappeared from Canadian waters as a direct result of overexploitation some years ago, and as far as I know, the stocks have never recovered. Similar things are happening all over the planet. The seas are being violated by fleets of fishing boats that use high technology to locate shoals of fish and then catch everything they can before processing it in factory ships and heading for the next area to be targeted. It's fishing on an industrial scale, and it's unsustainable. If the fish disappear from the seas, there will be calamitous effects for you humans, but not only for you. As creatures sharing this planet, we are all interdependent, and we need to protect every living thing we possibly can – the plants, the fungi, the insects, the reptiles, the birds and the mammals (and any other living thing I may have forgotten to mention). We need biodiversity and must do our utmost to avoid the further extinction of species. It's been estimated that thirty species a day are going extinct. Thirty species every day! Now, to its credit, Britain has signed up to the Convention on Biological Diversity Treaty, as has every other country in the world…well, not quite! Because, as you may know, there are a couple of countries which either haven't signed up, or haven't ratified. At least, that was the case when I last checked. And they are, in ascending order of population, The Vatican and... the United States of America. Well, The Vatican – The Holy See: no comment! But the United States! Now ladies and gentlemen, you don't need me to tell you that for some considerable time senior British politicians have been very fond of telling us that we have a special relationship with America; they claim that we are the closest of allies so, if that's the case, shouldn't we be putting pressure, however subtle, on our close friends to do the right thing and ratify! It's not in my power, as a mere owl, just another British bird, to influence American politicians, but maybe some of you, as parliamentarians, could send a few emails across the Atlantic to your opposite numbers over there to encourage them to add a rubber stamp to the signature, indicating ratification. After all, isn't that what friends are for – to look after each other and point each other in the right direction for the common good?'

Owl paused and stared into the faces of his audience. The MPs were not sure whether he had finished his speech or not, so the member who had stood up to welcome them when they had entered the room stood up again and thanked Owl for getting the proceedings underway with his very clear presentation. He then invited contributions from his fellow MPs. Owl looked surprised, but whether he was surprised at being thanked, or surprised at being interrupted before he had finished (if indeed he hadn't finished), or whether it was neither of these things is very difficult to say, because the permanent expression on Owl's face, in common with the rest of his species, is one which looks very much like surprise. Presumably, it's those big, round eyes fixed straight ahead that create this impression, but one thing's for sure, and that is if you ever see an owl that doesn't look surprised it probably isn't an owl at all!

One of the MPs took the opportunity to stand up in order to say his piece. Mr Fox turned a page in his notebook and held his pencil at the ready.

'Fellow members of this house and distinguished guests,' the MP began. 'As my colleague said, Mr Owl has given us an excellent start to our discussion and I, too, would like to express my thanks for his words. He made many interesting points, some of which are incontrovertible facts while others we may care to consider at this morning's meeting.'

Kingfisher looked at Blackbird, hoping that her friend would explain what "incontrovertible" meant, but there was no time, for the MP was pressing on. Blackbird just stretched out his wing so that it touched Kingfisher's feathers in a gesture of friendship and solidarity. Blackbird himself was finding that he needed to concentrate to follow what was being said.

'The first point I would like to make,' said the MP, 'is that the extinction of species is something that has always gone on. If species cannot adapt to new conditions it's always been the case that they will go under, they will disappear, they will have no place and no purpose in what we choose to call the grand scheme of things. As Mr Owl rightly said, this country supports the idea of biodiversity, as evidenced by its having joined up to the international treaty, but we have to be realistic, we can't save every species that's under threat. Successful species will change with the times and survive and prosper. Allow me to give a couple of examples from your own world of birds.'

Rachel and Rook exchanged glances, Kingfisher and Blackbird pricked up their invisible ears, Owl looked up at the ceiling and the cuckoo continued to fidget with his feathers. Mr Fox was still busy with his pencil and pad.

'Consider the magpie,' said the MP, scrutinising the faces of his plumed audience to see if the mention of the magpie produced a reaction. He thought he detected a look of distaste on the face of Blackbird and perhaps a slight cringe from the cuckoo, but he couldn't be sure in either case.

'The magpie,' he went on, 'was a bird of the countryside when I was a boy. It was rarely seen in suburban gardens, for it could find all the food it required in the fields and around the farms. Now, however, as farming practices have changed, magpies have also changed, and although some of them can still be seen in their traditional haunts the species has become a very visible part of the community of town and city dwellers. It has successfully moved into the urban setting, rather like its four-legged counterpart, the fox.' Editor-in-chief Mr Fox's notepad fell noisily to the floor at this moment and the MP turned and nodded to him, as if to congratulate him personally on the adaptability and triumph of his species.

'I pity the other town dwellers,' Blackbird sang quietly to Kingfisher. 'The magpie isn't just very visible. It's also horribly audible, and its habits are just about as unappealing as those of the fox, urban or rural.'

Kingfisher wasn't sure what "audible" actually meant, and "urban" and "rural" were words she wasn't too confident about either, but she could tell from Blackbird's tone that the magpie was not his favourite bird.

'My other example is the collared dove,' said the MP, seemingly impressed with his own ornithological expertise.

'The collared dove was unknown in Britain before the war and now there are almost a million nesting pairs. They are a real success story, collared doves. You can find them everywhere.'

'And more's the pity,' croaked Rachel to Rook. 'There can't be a bird in the land with a more irritating call than the collared dove,' she went on, as if the croak of a rook was the sweetest sound known to Nature.

The MP continued with his theme.

'The collared dove and the magpie are opportunistic, and that's the secret of their success. They notice when things are not going their way and they look for better places in which to operate. When they find them, they move in and make themselves at home, changing their habits where necessary and thriving. That's what I like in life, those who see a chance and grab it.'

'Whatever the consequences for others!' croaked Rachel to her uncle. 'I don't think I like this particular human very much, do you?'

'I don't think I like *any* humans very much,' he replied, true to form.

Whether the rooks liked him or not, the MP had not yet had his say. Well not all of it anyway, because he was in the process of taking a deep breath in preparation for his next point.

'My next point,' he said, 'concerns the sea. Our friend Mr Owl made reference to the oceans of the world and expressed his worries about their future. Again, I refer you to opportunism – just as relevant to the swimmers in the water as to the flyers in the air. See a chance and take it, that's my motto, and it's also the motto of the sarcastic fringehead,' he exclaimed with a triumphant gesture.

'The *what*?' said the visiting birds' local MP, speaking for the first time in the meeting. His face was a perfect mix of bewilderment and mirth. So far he had been following things closely and he'd been intrigued by Owl's excellent performance and well pleased with the remarks from his fellow parliamentarian. But "sarcastic fringehead"! Could his colleague possibly be serious? Mr Fox looked perplexed.

'The sarcastic fringehead,' repeated the speaker. 'Yes, it does exist. There really is a fish with such an unlikely name, but I haven't brought it into the discussion because of its exotic title. No, I refer to it simply because, like the magpie and the collared dove, it's an opportunist and it's clever. Now, without wishing to give the impression that I condone the dumping of all kinds of refuse in the sea, a practice which has always gone on, as far as I can tell, I would draw your attention to the fact that our friend the sarcastic fringehead sees an opportunity where others just see a problem. The things that humans have thrown into the sea – buckets, old lobster pots, and even discarded oil cans are used by the sarcastic fringehead to make a home for himself. This wonderful sounding fish actually makes its home in the detritus that we have tipped into the ocean. What a brilliant example this fish is setting to other species. Instead of giving up and going extinct, it seizes the moment and takes advantage of every opportunity that presents itself!' The MP had clearly done his research into the lifestyle of the sarcastic fringehead and found it difficult not to share a few more details with his wide-eyed audience. 'The male sarcastic fringeheads,' he continued, 'will defend their bucket homes, and compete for the best territories (as well as the most desirable females) by pushing their open mouths together. The male with the biggest mouth wins!'

'Just like male MPs, I suspect!' croaked Rachel to her uncle. He nodded without hesitation.

'Now, dear colleagues and guests, allow me to address some of the specific items listed by our friend, Mr Owl, in his splendid speech. He referred to the huge growth in the human population in recent times, and I must congratulate him on the accuracy of the statistics he quoted. He was quite correct in stating that the number of humans on the planet by the end of this century is expected to be about ten billion, but that should not be a cause for concern.'

All the birds, and even some of the other MPs, looked at each other with expressions that could only be described as showing concern – concern at the prospect of ten billion humans in the world, but perhaps more poignantly, concern at the lack of concern of their speaker. How could he be so complacent, when everyone knew that millions were malnourished and hungry even as he spoke, and two hundred thousand extra mouths were coming into the world every day! Was this man living on the same planet as everyone else, or was he just being deliberately provocative?

'Allow me to explain,' he went on.

'I wish you would,' croaked Rook, under his breath.

'I know that ten billion souls sounds like a lot, but by the beginning of the next century, that number is expected to level out and then decline. You see, we know the answer to the problem of population growth. We have the solution and we have things under control.'

'So, what is the answer, what is the solution?' Rachel interrupted, impatient with this pompous, bumptious man.

'The answer is simple,' he said, shrugging off the interruption. 'It's the education of women. Education in general, of course, is a good thing. But there is a direct correlation between the education of women and a significant decline in the birth rate. We've seen it in prosperous western countries for a long time, we've seen it more recently in Asia and we see it everywhere, once women become educated and learn about family planning and begin to take control of their own lives. Let me give you one country as an example. In Iran, in the nineteen sixties, most women had seven or eight children. Now it's typically one or two, just like in the west. And the reason is that Iranian women today are as well-educated as the men and as well-educated as westerners. Simple. Educate girls and save the planet!'

The MP paused and drank from a glass of water on a table beside where he was standing. He wiped his lips and took another deep breath, indicating that his simple solution to over-population was not the end of his message. Mr Fox turned another page of his notebook and also appeared to fill his lungs.

'Now, dear friends,' said the MP. 'If I remember correctly our first speaker, Mr Owl, began by telling us that bees and bumblebees were in decline because of loss of habitat. I believe he specifically mentioned the lack of clover fields. Well, there may be some truth in his assertion, but it's certainly not the whole picture and nothing has yet been proved. The experts themselves are divided, and in most cases puzzled, by the bee problem. Loss of habitat may be a factor in their decline, and the use of chemicals on the land may be another, but bees are under attack from the European foulbrood bacterium, and there's also the matter of a certain parasite, the varroa mite, which is killing off bees in continental Europe as well as here and in the United States. Scientists are working as hard as they can to get to the bottom of the problem, so we humans are certainly not complacent about it, and we are well aware of the vital role bees play in the food production process.'

At this point, Rook indicated a desire to speak, and the MP gave way.

'I've heard that in this country,' croaked Rook, 'the only bee to be doing relatively well these days is the urban bee, and that would seem to indicate that habitat and chemicals and insecticides are in fact key elements in the fate of all the other bees.'

'What exactly do you mean by that?' asked the MP, who was surprised and disturbed to find himself asking a bird for clarification of a point of discussion.

'What I mean is that the urban bee gets its nectar from city gardens, which are generally free of chemicals, and which provide a whole range of flowers, unlike the limited variety of crops we tend to find in the countryside, and the lack of meadows with wildflowers which used to be such a feature of the English landscape. The farmers of today are killing the countryside and decimating the wildlife.'

'Now hang on a minute,' said the MP, whose cheeks were beginning to turn quite a bright shade of pink. Rook's intervention had caught him off-guard and its accusatory tone was not entirely to his liking. 'As I said a moment ago, we are not sitting back and just letting the bees die. We are working on the problem and we do care.'

'Well, as I see it,' croaked Rook, 'this whole business with the bees is just one more example of you humans interfering with nature and not bothering about the consequences until you are directly affected. The only reason you care about the bees is because if they die you've lost the best pollinators of your crops – your apple trees and the like. You humans are selfish and always have been. You didn't care about the canaries that died in your coal mines. You weren't concerned about the carrier pigeons which were shot down carrying messages over the trenches in your wars, or the horses that died in the same wars. It's always the same. Use the animals for your own benefit. Put the hens in cages to produce eggs for your breakfasts. Catch the fish in your rivers for sport. Breed the cows to have udders so big they can hardly walk. Breed bulldogs until their faces are so flat, they can barely breathe. It just goes on and on.' Rook paused before releasing his final salvo:

'And one more thing: you said that you know the answer to the problem of the human population and that all will be fine in the end. There's just one small item you failed to mention, which is that consumerism is a bigger problem even than the size of the population. All the impoverished people in the world want to live the sort of lives you live in Britain and in the west, which means that even if the population eventually comes down, consumption will continue to rise. Just to take one example, massive amounts of water are needed to produce cotton for clothes, and advertisers and producers keep encouraging humans to buy more and more clothes, not because they need them, but for reasons of fashion and vanity and narcissism. Water is too precious a resource to be wasted on clothes that aren't even needed. It can't go on!

It isn't sustainable. The planet can't take it! The planet that you're overheating with your greenhouse gas emissions – it can't take it! You're changing the climate, you're melting the ice-caps and thawing the permafrost, you're causing heat-waves, forest fires, floods. You're ruining our planet, and things have got to change! And soon! Very soon! Very soon, indeed!

The MPs looked shocked at Rook's outburst. Owl and Blackbird looked embarrassed. Kingfisher looked as pretty as ever and the cuckoo looked around the room, much as he had done all morning. Mr Fox looked as if he was getting some good copy for "The Bugle". Rachel approved of what her uncle had said, but would have preferred it if he had chosen to express his sentiments in a slightly more respectful manner. However, Rook was Rook, and he was her uncle, so she quietly congratulated him for his straightforwardness and honesty. Their local MP stood up and politely suggested they might all have a moment or two of reflection before the discussion resumed. He had a whispered word with his colleague, whose face had by now become quite red, and it appeared that they agreed to hand the floor to the birds for the next few minutes so that more views could be aired. Owl had had his say, and so had Rook. Kingfisher demurred and Blackbird said he was happy to leave the debating to others, so now it was Rachel's turn. (The cuckoo was still considered to be something of an outsider, and possibly a bit of a loose cannon, too, so it didn't even occur to any of the birds to invite him to speak.) He didn't seem to notice, and it probably wouldn't have bothered him if he had! Rachel awaited her invitation to address the meeting, and after a couple more minutes her local MP walked over and asked her to make her contribution.

'Friends,' she began, hoping that this form of address might win back some of the MPs her uncle may have alienated, 'we have heard that recent practices seem to be responsible for changes to our environment and risks to our ecosystem, but modern technology has also given us useful tools for monitoring those very changes and assessing those risks. For example, surveys of the natural world are much more accurate and wide-ranging than anything we had in the past, so we should be thankful that we now have a great deal of up-to-date information about the state of the planet as a whole, as well as data about Britain and even statistics based on observations at quite a local level. All this helps us to quantify the risks identified and gives us unprecedented opportunities to attempt to rectify some of the things that have gone wrong and to make realistic plans for the future, in order to minimise the hazards and give our planet the best chance for its future health and sustainability.'

'Doesn't she croak well!' piped Kingfisher quietly into Blackbird's ear. Blackbird nodded.

'It'll be those years at Cambridge University. That's what it'll be,' he sang, equally quietly, into Kingfisher's ear. He then leaned across and sang very softly into Rook's ear:

'She's a born orator, your niece. You must be very proud.'

'I know,' croaked Rook in as hushed a tone as a rook can manage. 'In an earlier age, she'd probably have been an itinerant preacher. She's already wearing the uniform, isn't she?'

'Just think,' sang Blackbird, 'if John Wesley could travel a quarter of a million miles on a horse spreading the word of the Lord, how many miles could your Rachel have covered on a wing!'

'And a prayer,' croaked Rook, quick as a flash. A bit too quick for Blackbird, it seemed.

'Sorry?' sang Blackbird.

'On a wing and a prayer,' came the response, half croaked, half chuckled, and it shouldn't really come as a surprise that half a croak plus half a chuckle equals one choke, which is precisely what happened. Rook spluttered and choked with laughter at his own wit, and it was just one of those unfortunate things that the word "choke" was already in the dictionary because if it hadn't been, Rook (or his creator, at least) could have claimed it as a portmanteau word and might have joined the esteemed company of Charles Dodgson, aka Lewis Carroll, whose "chortle" (chuckle + snort) had ensured his immortality, even without Alice, the Cheshire Cat or the Dodo.

Rachel was unaware of these muted little conversations and didn't even hear her uncle's self-inflicted choking which, mercifully for him, was quickly brought under control. She was far too busy getting on with the serious business of delivering her maiden speech in Parliament to be distracted by anything, even the antics of her own uncle. She continued:

'If I may, I would like to draw your attention to a recent report about the state of Nature in Britain. As you probably know, much of this country was once covered by woodland. At the present time, the figure is just thirteen per cent, a situation that has not significantly changed in the last fifty years, and several of our best-loved trees are now under threat from a range of diseases, some of them apparently brought here on imported saplings. In that same fifty-year period, sixty per cent of British animal and plant species have declined. In 1966 there were two hundred and ten million birds nesting in the UK. Now there are one hundred and sixty-six million, a decline of forty-four million! Birds reliant on farmed land, like turtle doves, lapwings and cuckoos have seen a significant decrease in numbers.'

The cuckoo, upon hearing himself named in this way felt a sudden rush of self-consciousness course through his entire body, from the tip of his beak to the ends of his claws, and he attempted to tuck his head under his wing in embarrassment. Some of the MPs noticed, nudged each other and smiled, knowingly. Mr Fox didn't miss a thing. It all went into his notes.

Rachel went on:

'Experts are convinced that these decreases in bird populations are largely due to changes in the British landscape, with less habitat in which birds can feed and make their nests.'

The MP who had spoken earlier stood up and interrupted.

'With respect, you are giving us a one-dimensional picture here. I happen to have read the same report, and it says that our farmers are extremely interested in wildlife and are trying to help by encouraging and protecting the wildlife on their land. The report also points out that there are otters in many of our rivers where there were none a few years ago; sea eagles, red kites and even cranes have been re-introduced, so I suggest you should be a little less selective with your statistics and a bit more positive in your approach to the subject.'

'I don't deny the good news,' Rachel replied. 'I applaud it, but these are drops in the ocean. The hedgehog population in this country has gone down by 50 per cent since the year 2000. In the 1950s there were about 30 million hedgehogs in Britain. Now there are just over a million! Butterflies, moths and beetles have all been in decline for the last fifty years, and the number of turtle doves has reduced by ninety-three per cent! And not only that! You humans have nine or ten million pet cats in this country alone, and it's estimated that between them they kill at least fifty million British birds every year. You may not be aware of this, but cats have been blamed for the global extinction of thirty-three species, so isn't it about time you kept your pets indoors at night, and that you MPs legislated for a collar with a bell to be put around every British cat's neck to give us birds and some of the small mammals a better chance of survival?'

Rachel halted for a moment, hoping that her direct challenge to the MPs might give them pause for thought. She went on:

'A few minutes ago, my uncle mentioned the huge amount of water needed to grow cotton for clothes. As you know, without water there would be no life on the planet, and it seems to me that this precious resource is being squandered. I recently learned that it takes thirteen thousand litres of water to produce one kilogram of grain-fed beef. That being the case, you humans will have to think about making some drastic changes to your lifestyles, to what you actually put into your mouths, if there's to be enough water to go around.'

'Now then, now then,' said the MP. 'We can bandy figures about all day, but I just don't accept this hysteria which you and many like you are trying to whip up. It's scaremongering of the worst kind. Of course there are problems in the world. There always have been and there always will be, but I simply don't accept that the planet is in crisis. We humans are an ingenious species and we're perfectly capable of finding solutions, as we always have in the past. As I said before, the other species will have to adapt and then they'll prosper, just like us.'

Rachel was about to burst with indignation, as was her uncle, but the MP was already in full flow and evidently determined to finish what he was saying.

'There's no place in this world for stick-in-the-muds,' he went on. 'Never has been! My slogan has always been "Carpe diem!" which I'm happy to translate for you, my feathered friends. It means: "Seize the opportunity!"'

Rachel could contain herself no longer and stared the MP directly in the eye.

'That,' she croaked, 'is precisely the problem. You humans have always seized the opportunity and devil take the hindmost. That's what's got us into the mess we're in now. You've exploited the planet without giving any consideration to those who share it with you and without thinking of the future. "Carpe diem" may sound fine to you, but I, too, happen to be acquainted with that phrase, and I'm also aware of the rest of it – the part you failed to quote.'

The MP looked startled. In fact, he looked dumbfounded. A bird that was familiar with a Latin phrase! Whatever next! Mr Fox held his pencil at the ready, determined not to miss anything.

Rachel paused and every eye was fixed on her. The room was as silent as an abandoned bird-box. Even the cuckoo was looking at her, wondering what on earth she was going to say, and amazed at her poise and confidence in confronting this human, this man, this puffed-up Member of Parliament.

'The quotation is as follows: "Carpe diem, quam minimum credula postero",' Rachel croaked in an accent worthy of Horace himself. 'And I'm happy to translate for you, my clothed friends, and for the cuckoo. It means: "Seize the day, trusting as little as possible in the future". What it *doesn't* mean is: "Enjoy today, grab whatever you want and don't give a damn about tomorrow", which is the interpretation most of you humans seem to live by. No, what Horace meant when he wrote those lines more than two thousand years ago was that you should act today in order to make tomorrow better, because you never know what problems might be in store. It's not that different from our well-known saying: "The early bird catches the worm", which doesn't mean: "Grab the worm and let all the other birds die of starvation!" It means that if you start something early, you have a better chance of success. So, my friends, to put all this into the context of our debate, the advice must be that instead of ransacking the planet today, we should start planning for its recovery and a healthier future for it.'

The MP took a handkerchief from his pocket and wiped his brow. He screwed up his eyes and turned towards Rachel.

'Let me tell you something,' he said, feigning a conspiratorial tone. He leaned forward so that his face, still ruddy, was close to Rachel's beak. There was a thin, unconvincing smile on his lips. 'I don't wish to offend, but I must say that you are beginning to bore me, what with your classical quotations and your endless statistics. You sit there on your perch preaching at us as if you and your mates are the custodians of the planet, with all the answers and all the solutions. What I'd like to know is, how is it that you birds are so well-informed about everything? Where do you get all your facts and figures from? How come you know so much?'

Before Rachel could open her beak to answer, Blackbird flew up from his perch and landed on the back of the MP's empty chair.

'I'll tell you how Rachel and Rook and Owl are so well-informed,' he sang in a strong, confident voice. 'Unlike you humans, we birds have been twittering and tweeting for millions of years, keeping in touch with each other and exchanging information. And of course, we now have the Internest, the Bird Wide Web, which keeps us up-to-date with everything – well, those of us who have nests, of course.' He shot a quick glance at the cuckoo, who was the only one among them who wasn't online. No nest, no Internest! Simple as that!

'Huh,' went the MP, lost for words for the first time all morning. Mr Fox was still scribbling away, never at a loss for words.

The member who had shown the visitors to their perches at the beginning of the session now stood up and walked over to them.

'Ladies, gentlemen and guests, I think we have probably gone as far as we usefully can this morning,' he said. 'I note that tempers have become a little frayed, on both sides, but I don't think that's necessarily a bad thing. It indicates that we are dealing with very serious matters which have implications for all of us and for those we represent. When the stakes are high, as I believe they are in this instance, it's inevitable that passions will be aroused and feathers ruffled (if you'll pardon the expression), and although respect may sometimes have taken second place to conviction, that's not something we should dwell on. The important thing is that we have met at all and have had this opportunity to exchange views and see where the others are coming from. My hope is that this will be the first of many meetings. We should now be in a position to build on whatever common ground we can establish, with a view to improving the world, if not for ourselves, at least for our children, grandchildren and the future generations of all species. I would very much like to thank you six birds for making the journey from your homes to the Palace of Westminster and for sharing your thoughts, ideas and concerns with us. I'm sure I speak for all my colleagues when I say that we have been hugely impressed with your knowledge of the environmental issues at stake and with the robust manner in which you have put your case. We will keep in touch and move on from this first chapter so that further chapters may follow, and the benefits of cooperation rather than confrontation will become evident to us all. Thank you again.'

Owl flew across to join Blackbird on the back of the chair. He fluffed up his feathers, always a good indicator that he was about to pronounce:

'Ladies and gentlemen, it has been a privilege to come to Parliament and to be given this opportunity to debate with you today. It's clear that there are significant differences between us but, as has just been said, we must strive to identify areas where we can agree, so that a plan of action can be drawn up and progress made towards a common goal. It's in all our interests to play our part in protecting the planet and to help sustain all the beautiful, interesting and diverse species which constitute life on earth. We would like to thank you for your hospitality and we will be inviting you to a surprise event near our home sometime in the autumn. We hope you will be able to attend and we look forward to entertaining you. In the meantime, we will keep communications open so that ideas can be exchanged between us, with a view to arranging further meetings, which we hope will be positive, productive and ambitious. Thank you.'

With that, the meeting was over, Mr Fox added his last full stop and put down his notepad and pencil. The birds were invited to sit on the tea trolley and were then escorted to the main entrance by their local MP, who congratulated them on their spirited performance and wished them a pleasant return flight.

As soon as they were out of the building Owl found himself surrounded by his five friends, all of whom were clamouring to discover the mystery of the surprise event which he had promised to the MPs.

'What's the event, what's the surprise?' piped an excited Kingfisher. 'Tell us! Please tell us! Please! Do tell us!' she pleaded.

'What on earth do you have in mind?' croaked Rook, wondering how these unhelpful parliamentarians could possibly deserve any surprise event from them. 'You thanked them for their hospitality, but we didn't even get a drink of water, let alone a peck to eat. They are a despicable group of humans and I can't believe that you are planning to give them some kind of treat, unless, of course, you're planning a trick…an ambush maybe, taking hostages and demanding action on First Aid treatment for the planet by way of a ransom. Is that what you're thinking of?'

Owl was horrified at the wicked way Rook's mind was working and he said he wouldn't answer until they reached home.

They set off from London in a westerly direction, flying into a strong headwind. They flew in pairs, Rachel and Rook, Blackbird and Kingfisher, and Owl and the cuckoo. Strictly speaking, Owl and the cuckoo didn't really constitute a pair, because although they flew more or less side by side most of the time, they completely ignored each other's presence, each preferring to keep his own counsel. Rachel and Rook, on the other hand, were busily croaking away to each other all the way home, while Blackbird and Kingfisher were similarly engaged in conversation throughout the flight. They talked about all sorts of things – their impressions of London, the morning in Parliament, the surprise event for the MPs (whatever it was to be), and lots more besides. At one point, as they were leaving the suburbs and seeing the comforting sight of green once again Kingfisher suddenly remembered Rachel saying that she'd translate her Latin phrase for the humans and for the cuckoo.

'Why did she say "and for the cuckoo"?' she asked Blackbird.

'Because the cuckoo once said that he wasn't interested in Latin. He said that dead languages were of no use to a modern bird like a cuckoo.'

'Oh, I see. But it's not only the cuckoo who doesn't understand Latin, you know,' piped Kingfisher. There was silence from Blackbird, who just kept looking ahead, concentrating on flapping as strongly and steadily as he could into the blustery wind.

'I don't,' piped Kingfisher in a plaintive sort of way.

'You don't what?' sang Blackbird.

'I don't understand Latin, either,' piped Kingfisher, as if she wanted sympathy or consolation from her older friend.

Blackbird was a sensitive sort of bird, and despite his struggle with the wind, he was able to respond in just the right sort of way.

'Oh, don't worry,' he sang, 'Latin is hardly taught these days, so there aren't many of your generation who know any at all.'

'But I do know Greek,' piped Kingfisher, perhaps a hint of pride colouring her words.

'Do you?' sang Blackbird. 'Tell me more!'

'Well, I don't speak it fluently or anything, and I don't really know the alphabet, but...'

'So, what *do* you know, and how did you learn it?' Blackbird was intrigued.

'Well, you remember after last Christmas when I was teaching Owl to skim along the river and he was teaching me to hunt in the woods at night?'

'You mean the new exchange of Christmas presents? Of course I remember.'

'Well,' piped Kingfisher, 'Owl taught me some Greek one afternoon when we were down by the river. It was a beautiful day, and the river was glistening and sparkling in the sunlight, and Owl suddenly said that it reminded him of the halcyon days of his youth.'

'Yes...' sang Blackbird, 'and...?'

'And that was it,' piped Kingfisher.

'What do you mean "that was it"?

'Well, I said I didn't know what "halcyon" meant, and he said it was an Ancient Greek word, and it meant a time when he was very happy.'

'Yes?' sang Blackbird.

'Well, that's it, really,' piped Kingfisher.

'Oh, I see,' sang Blackbird. But there are lots of Classical Greek words in English. Words like "phobia", you know, when you're afraid of something…like hydrophobia – a fear of water, or arachnophobia – a fear of spiders…things like that.'

'How could *anyone* be afraid of water, or spiders?' piped an incredulous Kingfisher.

'Oh, it's not us, it's humans,' sang Blackbird, reassuringly.

'Oh, I see. Anyway, "halcyon" means "kingfisher" in Ancient Greek…that's what Owl told me, so that's what I know.'

'I didn't know "halcyon" meant "kingfisher",' sang Blackbird. 'That's so lovely. You must be really proud to fly around representing such a beautiful word, just knowing that you're a "halcyon".' Blackbird was silent for a while, then he suddenly sang: 'I wonder what owl means?'

'You wonder what Owl means when he says what?' piped Kingfisher, clearly puzzled.

'No, I mean, I wonder what the *word* "owl" means. Do you think it's Classical Greek, like "halcyon"?'

'No,' piped Kingfisher, 'I asked him that when he told me all about "halcyon", and he said that "owl" comes from Latin. I think he said it was "ulula" in Latin.'

'That's rather nice, too,' sang Blackbird. '"Halcyon" is definitely my favourite, but "ulula" sounds soft and gentle and musical.'

'A bit like Owl on a good day,' piped Kingfisher, 'but definitely not when he's hunting, or in a bad mood,' she added.

They both laughed.

'And then Owl told me about cuckoo,' piped Kingfisher.

'What about cuckoo?'

'He said "cuckoo" is just an imitation of the sound it makes.'

'Well that must be the same for the Latin word for "owl" – "ulula", don't you think?' sang Blackbird. 'When Owl's calling in the night, he makes that sort of sound.'

'Yes, now that you say it,' piped Kingfisher. 'I hadn't thought about it before, but I'm sure you're right.'

'So, what about rook?' sang Blackbird.

'What about Rook?' piped Kingfisher.

'I mean, what the word "rook" means?' sang Blackbird, amused at the confusion the conversation was causing, but suddenly quite curious about the origins of their names.

'I don't know,' piped Kingfisher, who was also beginning to acquire an interest in etymology, though she didn't know it was called that, of course. 'I'll tell you what, why don't we catch up with Owl and ask him?'

They did, and Owl said that "rook" came from the Anglo Saxon "hroc", which in turn came from the Gothic "hrukjan", which meant "to croak".

'Just another example of onomatopoeia,' said Owl in a rather dismissive tone. 'You know, where a word imitates the sound, like "cuckoo" and "bow-wow". In fact,' he went on, 'some linguists – another of those human subspecies, by the way…some of them think that human language started in this way, with people imitating animal calls and other natural sounds. They call the idea the "Bow-wow" theory of the origin of language.'

'How funny,' piped Kingfisher, who turned to Blackbird and added very quietly that she didn't think it would be wise to tell Owl that they thought his name in Latin was an imitation of his call, just like the cuckoo. 'He seems to look down on the idea,' she piped.

'He has a tendency to look down on a lot of things,' sang Blackbird, sotto voce, and in a wry tone.

They thanked Owl for the information, then dropped back to fly in his slipstream as well as that of the cuckoo, for the larger birds were better able to cope with the buffeting from the wind.

After several minutes of silence, apart, that is, from the sound of the wind and the flapping of wings, Kingfisher suddenly came out with another question:

'I wonder what "blackbird" means?' she piped in a tone that seemed to indicate that the question had been preying on her mind and was as genuine as any other question she'd ever asked.

Blackbird turned his head ever so slightly to look at his delightful young friend and to see if she was joking. But Kingfisher didn't really do jokes. It's not that she was too serious or reflective or cogitative for jokes. The truth is that she was none of those things. But she was not humourless either. It's just that jokes didn't really feature in her repertoire.

'What do you mean, "you wonder what 'blackbird' means"?' sang Blackbird, doing his best to sound sincere.

'I mean, we know what "cuckoo" means, and "rook" and "owl", but what does "blackbird" mean?' piped Kingfisher, sweet and innocent as ever.

'I think it probably means "black bird", from the colour of our bodies and heads,' sang Blackbird in as matter-of-fact a manner as he could manage.

'Oh, silly old me!' piped Kingfisher, who was certainly not old, but could, on occasions, be accurately described as silly.

All this chatting to each other was what constituted their in-flight entertainment on their long journey from London, and it was with a collective sigh of relief that they eventually saw their wood and their river and all the other familiar landmarks. They duly prepared for landing.

Once they were safely settled on the willow branch outside Kingfisher's riverside dwelling Owl agreed to tell them what the surprise event would be. He resumed the conversation they'd had outside Parliament when Rook had criticised the MPs for their lack of hospitality and unhelpful conduct. Owl continued exactly where they'd left off as if their journey hadn't happened at all.

'I agree with you, Rook,' said Owl, 'that the MPs were less than hospitable in the traditional sense of the word, but convention dictated that I should thank them, anyway. Perhaps the more astute among them may have wondered if my reference to hospitality was meant ironically, but...let them wonder, that's what I say. Perhaps it will give them pause for thought. As for the surprise event, I believe that by giving them a treat we'll be able to claim the moral high ground. If we are generous to them when they were conspicuously ungenerous to us it will surely be (forgive the expression) a feather in our caps, and it may well prove to be to our advantage in future dealings with them.'

'Please, Owl, tell us what the surprise is going to be?' piped Kingfisher, who was like a child on Christmas morning begging to be allowed to open a present before all the family were ready.

'Ah, yes, the surprise event! Well, it's not only going to be for the undeserving MPs. We will also invite the far more deserving students, who did know a thing or two about hospitality, and the councillors, who were, well, councillors!'

'What about the ornithologists?' said the cuckoo.

'And of course, the ornithologists,' said Owl, who may or may not have remembered to add them to the list without the cuckoo's timely prompt.

'Oh, Owl, you still haven't told us what it's going to be!' piped Kingfisher in a voice which, by now, had become more of a whimper than anything else. 'Please tell us!'

'The surprise event,' said Owl, 'is going to be a spectacle, a spectacular! Indeed, it will be a spectacular spectacle – something to behold, something which will make these humans realise how wonderful nature can be, even in their own backyard, so to speak. Even in this rather ordinary little corner of England. We'll show them. They'll be talking of it for the rest of their lives.'

Kingfisher had by now almost reached the depths of despondency, so exhausting was it to try and prize the information from Owl's beak, and that on top of all the air miles she'd travelled, and the nerve-racking hours facing the parliamentarians. She tried one last time:

'Owl, please Owl. Tell us. Please tell us about the surprise. What's it going to be?'

'Well,' said Owl, 'I'll have to confer with the protagonists first, because without them there won't be any spectacle, spectacular or otherwise,' he said.

Kingfisher was almost tearful.

'I don't know what "confer" means and I've no idea what a pro...progat...progatagist...'

'Protagonists,' said Owl. 'The protagonists are the main actors in a play or a film, or in this case a spectacle.'

'Oh, come on,' croaked Rook. 'For goodness' sake put her out of her misery. We can all keep a secret, can't we?' he croaked as he looked at each of his friends. 'We won't tell anyone until you give us the nod.'

'Alright,' said Owl, 'but you must all promise not to breathe a word about it to a soul. You mustn't tell a single bird or other woodland creature. And in particular, you mustn't tell a sparrow!'

'We promise,' they sang, piped and croaked in unison. Even the cuckoo agreed to keep his beak closed.

'Well,' said Owl, 'what I have in mind is the biggest, the most spectacular, the most exciting murmuration of starlings anyone has ever seen. Some of the humans will have seen the bizarre synchronised dancing of thousands of flamingos in nature programmes on TV, they may have seen massive shoals of sardines off the African coast performing their synchronised swimming to escape from the jaws of dolphins in David Attenborough's documentaries, and some of them will no doubt have noticed flocks of starlings flying about in the twilight, but none of them will have witnessed anything on the scale I'm envisaging. There will be more than a hundred thousand starlings swirling around the sky in perfect synchrony, spiralling up and coiling down again, wheeling and twisting as one through some mysterious instinctive signal that makes them seem like a single creature, willowy and lithe one moment, round and pliant the next, splitting into two then three or four groups before merging again into one, like a river that's been separated by a couple of islands suddenly joining up effortlessly into a single flow. These humans will have seen their Red Arrows doing aerobatics and flypasts, but they won't have seen anything to compare with this. Just picture it – a hundred thousand starlings flying wingtip to wingtip, and miraculously there won't be a single collision or false move. I promise, it will be a visual feast to rival any pageant or display you care to name, and it will provoke a jaw-dropping reaction from those humans lucky enough to be invited. And I'm willing to wager that among your good selves there will be many an open beak as you watch this awesome event. So, what do you think?'

'I think you'd better ask the starlings first, as you said,' croaked Rook with a smiley sounding croak.

'I think it sounds just perfect, 'piped Kingfisher. 'A brilliant idea! I'm so excited!'

'Wonderful scheme,' sang Blackbird.

'The starlings will do us proud,' croaked Rachel. 'I've often watched them doing their displays, and there's nothing like it. They're magic!'

'Looking forward to it,' said the cuckoo. 'Looking forward to it. Or rather, I would be, but by then I'll be sitting in the rainforest eating juicy, fat African caterpillars!'

Once life had settled down again, after the excitement of London and all the meetings with the various groups of humans, Owl started making plans for the starling spectacular. He decided to make contact with the

183

ornithologists so that they could play a part in the event. It seemed the right thing to do, since they had been instrumental in putting the birds in contact with the councillors and the students, and eventually, the MPs. Owl paid a visit to Mr Fox at the "Bugle", asking him to arrange a meeting with the ornithologists. Mr Fox was delighted to be involved, for his entire way of life and manner of doing business was concerned with establishing contacts, maintaining them and, if at all possible, making use of them in some way or other. He agreed to fix a meeting on condition that he would be invited to the event when it took place. Owl knew perfectly well that Mr Fox would be there whether or not he was invited, so he was more than happy to extend a formal invitation to him there and then.

At his meeting with the ornithologists, Owl suggested that on the evening of the spectacular, they might like to do the introduction for the benefit of the other humans, so that everyone would have some relevant background information before the starlings put on their show. The ornithologists said they would choose one of their number to represent them, and assured Owl that an appropriate introduction would be given.

The man they chose was someone who had done research into starlings and their behaviour so, when the day came, he was able to give lots of interesting facts and a few worrying figures. He pointed out that starlings, like many other British birds, were in decline and were, therefore, a cause for some concern. He was a very tall man with a bushy red beard. Kingfisher leaned over to Blackbird and quietly piped that she knew a wren and a goldcrest who would be more than happy, in fact, would probably give their right wing, to make their nest in such a fine growth of fibre. Blackbird laughed in agreement.

'After you have witnessed the murmuration of the starlings,' said the ornithologist as he rounded off his introduction on the day of the spectacular, 'you will, I am sure, be asking yourselves how such brilliant and precise co-ordination is possible with over a hundred thousand birds flying in such close formation.' He looked at his audience, who did, indeed, appear to anticipate that just such a question might occur to them.

'Well,' said the ornithologist, 'here are a couple of facts to bear in mind. The first is that every starling will be automatically monitoring the precise movements and changes in direction and speed of its seven nearest neighbours in the flight. The second equally important fact is that the starling's reaction time is ten times faster than that of an RAF fighter pilot! And finally, ladies and gentlemen, I would like to draw your attention to one of nature's subtleties. The starling is often perceived as a rather dull bird as far as its appearance is concerned, but that is far from the truth. Since we are blessed with a wonderful clear sunset this evening, I'd ask you to try and spot the brilliant iridescent sheen on the feathers of the birds when they fly close, as I'm told they will. You won't be able to distinguish all the shades of purple and green and blue as they flash past, but you will, I think, see them in a new light, in every sense of the word. Thank you, Mr Owl and your fellow birds for arranging this event. I'm confident that it will be a memorable evening for us all.'

The humans seemed to find the introduction entertaining and suitably informative, and the ornithologist was given a hearty round of applause. He joined his fellow ornithologists who, together with the councillors and the students and the MPs, were sitting on a bank at the edge of the wood, with the birds, except for the cuckoo, of course, perched above them in a fine oak tree. Mr Fox was sitting next to the MPs, with his trusty notepad and pencil at the ready.

Within a couple of minutes of the ornithologist finishing his introduction and taking his seat one of the students shouted 'Here they come!' And sure enough, here they came, all one hundred thousand of them. They put on the display of their lives, captivating their audience for over an hour. It was a ballet in the heavens, choreographed to perfection. It was as daring as it was beautiful – every bit as exciting and exuberant as Owl had promised. At times the mass of birds appeared to become plumes of smoke rising and curling up into the sky, and then they would hurtle back towards the ground, swaying this way and that, all the while changing shape, intricate, fluid – an elaborate work of art being created before everyone's eyes. It was, without doubt, an aesthetic masterpiece. There were gasps of wonderment when the murmuration passed particularly close, something which Owl had specifically requested.

'Fly as near to the spectators as you dare,' he'd said, 'so that they can hear the swish of your wings and feel the rush of the air as you dart past their faces in the cool of the evening.'

The entire performance was majestic, and all who were privileged to witness it would surely keep and treasure the memory for the rest of their lives. It was nature at its splendid best. Sublime!

Now we all know that a dog can't miaow and a cat can't bark, but it seems that a bugle can trumpet because, thanks to the efforts of Mr Fox, "The Woodland Bugle" loudly trumpeted the triumph of the starlings that evening. The starlings were stars, everyone said so, and after their magnificent pageant in the sky, things began to happen. For a start, the cats of England, instead of prowling the suburbs every night, were discovered to be sitting indoors – during the birds' nesting season, at least. They were mostly watching television on their owners' laps and, believe it or not, they were wearing collars with tinkly little bells. The humans gradually began to change their ways, too, as a result of which the birds made a decision to work more closely with them for the good of the planet.

Chapter Twelve

After some time, they managed to persuade a number of four-legged animals to join them in their co-operation with the humans. Their first recruit was Mr Fox. No surprise there, because he was always on the lookout for material for "The Bugle", and what could possibly be more newsworthy than saving the planet! Mr Fox wanted to be in on the act, making news as well as reporting it. In editorial after editorial he urged other animals to commit to the cause, and his efforts, combined with those of the birds, began to pay off. Before long all the animals in the wood had joined up and had pledged to spread the word beyond their own patch so that all the animals of Britain would eventually be involved in this ground-breaking project.

Several generations of humans lived and died before they succeeded in significantly reducing their own population. It took them even longer to get consumerism under control, but little by little, progress was made, the humans saw the folly of their ways and, working in harmony with the beasts and the birds, not just of Britain but of the whole world, they re-discovered that greater harmony with the entirety of nature that their ancestors had enjoyed. It took many, many generations of wood-mice and even more generations of woodlice before most of the planet's problems could be solved, but thanks to the pioneering work of Rook and Rachel, Blackbird, Kingfisher and Owl and the continuing work of their descendants, and the co-operation of the humans and their children and children's children and children's, children's children the tide was turned, the brink was avoided and the fate of the planet was ultimately determined not by the living things which walked on its soil and swam in its waters and flew in its air, but by the far greater forces that were to be found in the heavenly bodies of the universe. And the cuckoo? Oh yes, the cuckoo! Well, he fared much better than the dodo, for with the owls and the rooks and the rest he was there, and like them and like the humans, he witnessed the end of the world when the world itself was ready to end.

Or is that really what happened? The birds and the humans and all the other animals certainly did co-operate. They had meetings and more meetings, there were committees and resolutions, and ten-year plans and ambitious goals, and the humans did eventually manage to reduce their population, but did they really minimise their exploitation of the planet's resources? Did they really stop polluting the air and the water and the soil? Did they halt their greenhouse gases? Did they prevent plastic waste from getting into the food chain, and did they allow fish to live long enough to breed and maintain their numbers, so that everything was back in balance? Did they give the forests enough time to recover from the ravages of the logging industry? Did they stop killing rhinos for their horns and elephants for their tusks, tigers for their bones, sharks for their fins and pangolins for their scales, or did the poachers and the traders win in the end? Did animal parts ultimately prove more valuable than the animals themselves?

Did the humans make wars over access to water? Did they drop bombs on each other, causing whole areas of the world to be contaminated by radioactive fallout, killing millions of humans and animals alike? And did they allow the threatened species of wildlife to go unprotected until they became extinct? And is that what became of the cuckoo? Did he die out as a species, surviving only, perhaps, in some work of fiction, just as the poor old dodo only survived in the pages of Dodgson's (our friend, Lewis Carroll's) "Alice's Adventures in Wonderland"? Was that his fate, and if it was, how long did he survive in fictitious form before the humans also became extinct, with only themselves to blame?

THE END (Maybe)

Ingram Content Group UK Ltd.
Milton Keynes UK
UKHW022032120323
418334UK00005BA/336

9 781398 442580